TO CATCH A SPY

ALSO BY STUART M. KAMINSKY

TOBY PETERS MYSTERIES
Bullet for a Star
Murder on the Yellow Brick Road
You Bet Your Life
The Howard Hughes Affair
Never Cross a Vampire
High Midnight
Catch a Falling Clown
He Done Her Wrong
The Fala Factor
Down for the Count
The Man Who Shot Lewis Vance
Smart Moves
Think Fast, Mr. Peters
Buried Caesars
Poor Butterfly
The Melting Clock
The Devil Met a Lady
Tomorrow Is Another Day
Dancing in the Dark
A Fatal Glass of Beer
A Few Minutes Past Midnight

ABE LIEBERMAN MYSTERIES
Lieberman's Folly
Lieberman's Choice
Lieberman's Day
Lieberman's Thief
Lieberman's Law
The Big Silence
Not Quite Kosher

LEW FONESCA MYSTERIES
Vengeance
Retribution

PORFIRY ROSTNIKOV NOVELS
Death of a Dissident
Black Knight in Red Square
Red Chameleon
A Cold, Red Sunrise
A Fine Red Rain
Rostnikov's Vacation
The Man Who Walked Like a Bear
Death of a Russian Priest
Hard Currency
Blook and Rubles
Tarnished Icons
The Dog Who Bit a Policeman
Fall of a Cosmonaut
Murder on the Trans-Siberian Express

JIM ROCKFORD MYSTERIES
The Green Bottle
Devil on My Doorstep

NON-SERIES NOVELS
When the Dark Man Calls
Exercise in Terror

BIOGRAPHIES
Don Siegel: Director
Clint Eastwood
John Huston, Maker of Magic
Coop: The Life and Legend of Gary Cooper

OTHER NONFICTION
American Film Genres
American Television Genres (with Jeffrey Mahan)
Basic Filmmaking (with Dana Hodgdon)
Writing for Television (with Mark Walker)

TO CATCH A SPY

A TOBY PETERS MYSTERY

STUART M. KAMINSKY

An Otto Penzler Book

CARROLL & GRAF PUBLISHERS
NEW YORK

TO CATCH A SPY
A TOBY PETERS MYSTERY

Carroll & Graf Publishers
An Otto Penzler Book
An Imprint of Avalon Publishing Group Incorporated
161 William Street, 16th Floor
New York, NY 10038

First Carroll & Graf edition 2002
Second printing, August 2002

Library of Congress Cataloging-in-Publication Data is available.

ISBN: 0-7867-1023-3

Printed in the United States of America
Distributed by Publishers Group West

This one is for Angela and Barry Zeman.

AUTHOR'S NOTE

On April 18, 1947, King George VI awarded Cary Grant the King's Medal for Service in the Cause of Freedom, citing his "Outstanding service to the British War Relief Society." It has been widely believed, and Grant never denied, that since the late 1930s he had been working as a special agent for the British Intelligence Services. Several years later, a telegram from Sir William Stephenson, Head of British Security Coordination, confirmed Grant's role as a secret agent.

PROLOGUE

ONE GOOD THING about the war-time blackouts was that the lights of Los Angeles didn't wash away the stars at night. The stars and an almost half-moon gave enough light, but just enough, to keep us from crashing into scrub and trees at the top of Laurel Canyon above the reservoir.

Behind us the house was growing smaller, dimmer but still visible when I turned my head as I ran, knowing that someone with a gun and a willingness to use it was about twenty yards behind. I take that back. He was not just willing to use the gun. He was eager to use it or anything else lethal that he could lay his hands on.

I wasn't in bad shape for a man nudging the back end of his fifth decade, nursing a sore shoulder and a recently stitched head wound and some deep scratches. Or, to stop beating around the bush, which was literally what I was doing, I wasn't in bad shape for a forty-eight-year-old. I wasn't sure where we were running to. I knew what we were running from.

I turned my head to see how far behind our pursuer might be. I shouldn't have. I think I tripped over a rock. It might have been a tree stump. It doesn't matter. I sprawled, landed on my stomach, and lost my breath.

In front of me, my fellow potential prey heard my flop and came running back. He was in better shape than I was and not even panting.

"You all right, Peters?" he whispered, kneeling to help me up as he looked back toward our pursuer, who we could hear thrashing through the trees in our direction.

I tried to say something, but my lungs were empty. I shook my head. I'm not sure whether it shook up and down or sideways. I'm not sure my friend could see clearly what I was doing.

"We'd better keep moving," he said, pulling me up.

Something was wrong here. I was supposed to be protecting him. That's what I was getting paid for. Maybe, if we survived, I should consider giving him some of his money back.

"All . . . right," I gasped.

"Fine," he said, tugging at my elbow. "Which way do we go?"

I nodded into the dark, away from the guy behind us, away from the house we had left behind. Our pursuer was getting closer. He didn't sound as if he was avoiding the trees and bushes. He sounded as if he was plowing through them.

We ran. I was about a dozen feet behind, and if my client hadn't stopped suddenly, I would have run right past him into the canyon.

We stood at the rim and looked down into the empty darkness below us. There were glints of the moon off of a pool of water, and across the reservoir canyon I could make out a few dim dots of light from a ranger station on the other side.

To our left was the rim of the canyon. To our right was the rim of the canyon. Behind us . . . I didn't want to think of what was behind us. I didn't really want to think of what was in front of us, or to put it more accurately, what wasn't in front of us.

There was nothing to say. We both knew what had to be done.

"Come on," he said, going to his knees at the edge of darkness and feeling for something to grab hold of. I started forward as he disappeared behind hanging rock.

"Come on," he whispered from the blackness. "We can do it."

"I've got an idea," I said. "I hide up here. You make noise. He comes over the edge. I sneak up behind him and hit him with a rock."

"Do you see someplace up there to hide?" his voice came from below.

I looked around. The nearest cover was a lightning-struck tree too far back for me to get to before I came face-to-face with the man behind us.

"I'm coming," I said, getting to my knees and starting to make my way over the ledge.

"There's a firm bush by your right hand," he said below me. "And I'm on a narrow ledge."

I made my way over the rim of the canyon. His hand braced me. I had no idea how far down we would have to climb. I had a fairly good idea that I wasn't up to it. I spent time in the downtown Y working on the heavy and light bags and playing as much handball as I could with Doc Hodgdon, who was well over eighty and beat me regularly. That was the credit side. The debit side was that I had a trick back that gave out whenever it felt independently moved to torment me.

My client, however, was almost a decade younger than I was and in far better shape, a little over six-foot-one and about 180 pounds. I knew he had been a professional acrobat and had seen him do a standing back flip wearing a smile.

"Hug the wall," Cary Grant whispered, his left hand gripping my arm. "I don't think he can see us."

I was in no position to argue and, considering the depth of

blackness below us—and, I hoped, just above us—I was in no position to disbelieve.

That was before I looked up, heard a click, and saw the beam of a flashlight over our heads.

"Down," Grant whispered urgently.

"Where?" I whispered back.

The beam of light above was looking a lot brighter and closer.

"Find something to hold on to," said Grant. "Someplace to hide."

I moved my right foot carefully against the side of the canyon wall and slid it down, hoping for something solid, a rock, a crag, a branch, or bush. There was nothing there, and my grasp of whatever thin rocky overhang was definitely giving way.

"Slipping," I said, looking up and seeing just the outline of Grant's silhouette.

"Reach up," he said. "Grab my wrist."

"Your wrist?"

"My wrist. Did you see *Bringing up Baby*?"

I could think of better times and places to talk about movies, but I said, "Yes."

"The end," he said. "When the brontosaurus bones start to fall apart and I grab Kate Hepburn and pull her up to the platform."

"I remember it vividly," I said, feeling my fingers growing numb.

"I told her to grab my wrists," Grant said. "The way I was taught when I was learning to be an acrobat. It worked perfectly. I won't let you fall. Just reach up. I'll grab your wrist. You grab mine. I won't let you fall."

My choices were limited. I looked up, my cheek against the rough surface of the rock and dirt. Something scuttled across my right hand and down my arm under my sleeve. I was definitely not having one of my better days.

I lifted my eyes. The beam of the flashlight was close to the rim of the canyon now, just above where Grant was clinging tightly and firmly, I hoped, to something solid.

"Now," said Grant.

I let go with my left hand and reached in semi-panic into the darkness above. For an instant there was nothing and my left hand couldn't hold me. Then I felt Grant's hand firmly grasp my wrist as I grasped his. Mine was gritty and sweating. His hand seemed dry.

I dangled above nothingness, wondering who would be attending my funeral and who would pay for it. That was providing my body was found or anyone bothered to look for it.

I had better things to do, like trying to find something to hold on to with my left hand, but a headline flashed in front of me—one of those headlines from a Jimmy Cagney movie, where the front page comes flying toward you out of the darkness. The headline read: CARY GRANT DIES IN CANYON FALL. Then, when the front page was inches from my eyes, there was a small paragraph at the end of the front-page story with Grant's photograph three columns across. "Private detective Tony Peterson also dies in tragic accident."

I couldn't even get my own name right.

Grant started to pull me up. We weighed about the same. At forty, he was eight years younger, and, judging from what I had seen of him over the last week and what I was feeling now as he lifted me, he was a hell of a lot stronger.

I looked up into the beam of the flashlight. Just the beam. I couldn't see his face. I didn't have to. I knew who had chased us through the woods and to the end of the known world.

The beam hit Grant and illuminated his face. He was straining to hold me with one hand and to maintain his grip on the rock with the other.

The beam of light moved down. Our pursuer was leaning over or kneeling now.

"I can't hold much longer," Grant said apologetically.

From behind the circle of light, a hand reached down toward Grant's clinging fingers. It was a big hand, and it was definitely in the process of prying loose the actor's fingers.

I looked down. Man cannot fly. Man cannot, in spite of the belief of my mystical poet landlord, Jeremy Butler, levitate. I would grab as I fell. I might shout. Neither would hurt. Neither would help much. I'd go out as a minor footnote in the strange death of Cary Grant.

I had been hired to help the actor. It looked as if I had succeeded in getting him killed. As Grant's fingers were further pried from the rock, I had to admit that I was feeling a little sorry for myself. I had so many tacos left to eat, so many movies to see, so many mistakes left to make.

What the hell? Grant's fingers were definitely giving out.

"Sorry," he said.

I nodded. I'm sure he didn't see me.

CHAPTER 1

IT HAD STARTED five nights earlier. Friday, December 31, 1943. New Year's Eve. My landlady, Mrs. Plaut, had thrown a party to which she accepted no refusals or excuses. Irene Plaut, tiny, broomstick thin, almost deaf, and somewhere over eighty years old, was not a creature to whom one could say "no." She simply issued proclamations and expected them to be obeyed. In this case it had begun with a summons two weeks before the party being held at her boardinghouse on Heliotrope Street, two blocks off of Hollywood Boulevard.

She had painstakingly and in tiny letters handed out flowered invitations to her tenants and had given me a handful to deliver.

The invitations read:

> A PARTY CELEBRATING THE ARRIVAL OF THE NEW YEAR OF OUR LORD NINETEEN HUNDRED AND FORTY-FOUR WILL BE HELD AT THE HOME OF MRS. IRENE PLAUT ON DECEMBER THIRTY-ONE, NINETEEN HUNDRED AND FORTY-THREE. IT WILL COMMENCE AT THE HOUR OF EIGHT AND END AT THE HOUR OF TWELVE-THIRTY-SEVEN,

WHICH IS THE HOUR THE LATE MISTER WENT TO MEET OUR MAKER ON THIS SELF-SAME DATE TWENTY-FOUR YEARS AGO. FOOD AND REFRESHMENTS AND APPROPRIATE BEVERAGES WILL BE SERVED. APPROPRIATE DRESS AND BEHAVIOR IS EXPECTED.

IRENE ZENOBIA PLAUT

Mrs. Plaut had handed me the stack of invitations in little blue envelopes after we had one of our regular morning discussions about food stamps. This discussion particularly baffled me.

"There will be a new pork bonus from the Office of Price Administration after the start of the new year," she explained slowly. "Spare stamp number two in ration book four will be worth five points of fresh pork and sausage, not smoked or cured pork or bacon."

"Yes," I said, standing in her sitting room on the first floor and trying not to check my watch. Actually, there was no point in checking my watch. It had belonged to my father and was the only thing I had of his. It never told the correct time. Edgar Guest or Will Rogers or someone once said that even a stopped watch is right twice a day. My father's watch kept running but jumped back and forth in time. I once tried to have it fixed, but the watchmaker said he couldn't see anything wrong with it.

"It's jinxed," he had declared professionally. "Not the first one I've seen jinxed like that."

He charged me a quarter. I kept wearing the watch.

"Are you listening, Mr. Peelers?" Mrs. Plaut asked.

Mrs. Plaut had decided when I moved into her boardinghouse that my name was Tony Peelers and that I was a full-time exterminator and part-time book editor. These misconceptions were a combination of misunderstood conversations and Mrs. Plaut's unswerving hold onto whatever initial conclusions she drew. I had learned to go along quietly.

"I'm listening," I said. "Pork."

"Pork," she repeated. "This change will be good only from January two to January fifteen, which will be a Saturday. Spare stamp number one, which has been good for fresh and cured pork, will expire on January two."

"I see," I said, having no idea what she was talking about but understanding she wanted me to turn over some of my ration stamps to her. I had brought my ration books down from my room, anticipating this because Mrs. Plaut had awakened me at seven-thirty by opening the door to my room, mop in hand, and announcing, "We must not waste the day."

There were no locks on the rooms in Mrs. Plaut's boardinghouse. There was no need for an alarm clock, providing you wanted to get up no earlier than seven-thirty.

I had been lying on the mattress on the floor, wearing my boxer shorts and a bleary, unshaven look of semiconfusion on my battered face. I'm no beauty. My nose is almost flat, my hair is dark but showing more than a little gray. I'm compact, meaning I'm somewhere between five-eight and five-ten depending on where I measure myself. I look like a washed-up boxer who had ten too many fights. In my profession, private investigator, the look was perfect.

I had dressed quickly, rolled the mattress back on the bed, put on clean if slightly creased pants, and hurried to the only washroom on the floor to wash and shave. The other residents of Mrs. Plaut's were already downstairs, awaiting breakfast and me. Mrs. Plaut always waited until we were all seated in her small dining room before serving.

At breakfast that morning, Mrs. Plaut had handed out invitations like summonses. The first went to my closest friend, Gunther Wherthman, the less-than-four-foot-tall Swiss little person, who had once been in the circus and had appeared in *The Wizard of Oz*. Gunther made his living by translating documents, books, and articles from more than a dozen languages for publishers and the U.S. government. He took the invitation with a nod of his head and an adjustment of his perfectly pressed three-piece suit. Gunther wore a suit and tie and carefully polished shoes every day even though he worked at the desk in his room.

Other invitations were handed to Emma Simcox, a good-looking, lean woman in her forties, who worked in the office at the May Company. According to Mrs. Plaut, Miss Simcox was her grandniece. Mrs. Plaut's pallor was the color of mountain snow. Emma Simcox was definitely a light-skinned Negro. There was no sign of family resemblance, but Miss Simcox did call Mrs. Plaut "Aunt Irene."

Ben Bidwell, who smiled when he took the invitation, was a car salesman at Mad Jack's in Venice. He was about fifty, skinny, dark-haired, and one-armed. The lost arm went missing somewhere at Verdun. Emma Simcox was quiet and shy. Bidwell was either bouncy and full of bad jokes or so depressed that he couldn't talk.

We already had the beginning of a great New Year's Eve party.

Breakfast, as I recall, had consisted of coffee, orange juice, Eggs Garfield Surprise, and Spam covered with a pasty, gray layer of sauce. No one asked what was in the Eggs Garfield Surprise. No one wanted to know. It didn't taste bad.

Throughout our discussion of pork stamps, Mrs. Plaut's bird had squawked, making conversation just a little bit more difficult. Mrs. Plaut had not heard the bird, whose wide variety of screeches and sounds that resembled words could be heard throughout the house when she left her door open. She changed its name regularly, not because she kept forgetting but because, as she said so pithily, "Variety is the spite of life."

The bird's current name was Pistolero.

I had delivered the invitations dutifully to everyone, including my brother, Phil, and his family; my office landlord and friend, the poet Jeremy Butler and his wife, Alice Pallice Butler; my mechanic,

No-Neck Arnie; Sheldon Minck, D.D.S., inside of whose office at the Farraday Building I had my closet-with-a-window that served as my working address; Violet Gonsenelli, Shelly's secretary-receptionist; and Juanita, the bespangled sixty-plus-year-old soothsayer with a never-to-be-lost Bronx accent.

It promised to be quite a party.

For the next two weeks I went to my office, listened to Shelly tell me about his new plan to use high-speed water jets to clean teeth "just like fire hoses," and avoided making bets on any fights with Violet, whose husband, Rocky, was a promising middleweight whose career had been interrupted by the war. Rocky was serving somewhere in the Pacific. I had some minor work done on my Crosley by No-Neck Arnie, whose son was in uniform somewhere in Italy.

I had lunch almost every day at Manny's Tacos on the corner, listening to poetry Jeremy had written and doing my best to avoid Juanita, who always had something important to tell me about my future. Juanita was usually right, but what she told me never made much sense until after it happened.

As for work, I had one job for a week filling in at night for the house detective at the Roosevelt Hotel, and I did four days at Hy's For Him clothing store on Melrose. Someone had been getting away with suits again. I basically sat in my Crosley for hours outside of Hy's and tailed whoever came out looking bulky or carrying something that could hold a passable gabardine jacket. It took three days. The thief was one of Hy's new salesmen, a wounded war vet named Sidney, who walked with a limp and was reselling Hy's inventory to pay for a morphine habit he had picked up in the army.

Then came the day before the new year began. I had been at my office with nothing much to do except listen to the arguments of a trio of panhandlers who did something like living in the small, square, cluttered concrete lot five stories down below my open window. I looked at the photograph on the wall across from my desk. It wasn't far away. There was just enough room in the former storage room for my desk and two chairs for drop-ins or the occasional clients I was forced to meet here instead of someplace more impressive.

The photo on the wall was of me, my father in the middle, and my brother, Phil. Phil looked older than his fourteen years. I looked like a kid with a goofy smile who was not destined to grow up beautiful. At our feet was our German shepherd, Kaiser Wilhelm. My father, in his grocer's apron, wore a sad smile as he clutched his sons to him. My mother wasn't in the picture. She had died giving birth to me, which caused a lifelong resentment from my brother, who was now a Los Angeles police lieutenant.

On the wall to my left was a large painting, a woman holding two babies and looking down lovingly at them. The traditional-looking painting had been a gift from Salvador Dalí, a former client. I seldom told people the painting was by Dalí, and I only told those who asked and who I knew wouldn't believe me when I told them.

The *Los Angeles Times* lay open in front of me. Army bombers were hitting Jap bases in the Marshall Islands, particularly Kwaja. In Italy, the Fifth Army was on the Casino Road and battling in San Vittorio. They were on the way to Rome. Inevitably, but at a price, they would get there in a few weeks.

Mrs. Plaut had told me to dress "nicely" for the party, which was why, although I needed the money, I took my pay from Hy in the form of a lightweight gray seersucker. I called Anita to tell her I'd be picking her up at seven-thirty and told her about my new suit.

"What color?" she asked.

"Gray, seersucker."

"Let Gunther pick out your tie," she said.

I was going to anyway, but I said, "Okay."

I had known Anita since high school, had taken her to the prom, and had lost track of her for more than two decades, a marriage and divorce for each of us, a daughter for her. I had run into her at the Regal drugstore, where she worked behind the counter. We were comfortable together right away.

Anita was nothing like my ex-wife, Anne, who had left me because she wanted a husband not a kid who kept aging. Anne was a few years younger than me, with a beautiful dark face and full body and more style than I had ever deserved. She was married now to a B-movie star. I actually liked him. Anita was thin, blonde, and good-looking, particularly when she tried and wasn't worn out from a day of dishing out burgers, Cokes, and cole slaw.

I decided to reread the funnies and was just moving from "Brick Bradford" to "The Little King" when the phone call came through.

"There's a guy on the phone," Violet said. "Says he has to talk to you. Didn't give his name but did a rotten imitation of Cary Grant. Almost as bad as Dr. Minck's."

I picked up the phone.

"Toby Peters," I said.

"Cary Grant," he said. "A former client of yours, Peter Lorre, told me you'd be the right person to handle a delicate job."

"Peter Lorre," I said.

"Yes, I did *Arsenic and Old Lace* with him about a year ago. He mentioned your name. I asked some questions and here I am."

"And you're Cary Grant?"

"Born Archibald Alexander Leach in Bristol, England. Became a U.S. citizen two years ago and am now officially Cary Grant and in need of some very confidential help from a reliable investigator."

"Okay," I said. "Let's meet."

"How about tomorrow?" he said. "My wife's throwing a New Year's party tonight. I think it would be better if I came to your office. I don't want Barbara, my wife, knowing about this."

"Name the time," I said.

"How does eleven in the morning suit you?" he asked. "It will give us both plenty of time to sleep. I know I'll need it. My wife's parties go on most of the night."

"You have my address?" I asked.

"Yes."

"My office is modest," I said.

"That sounds like what I need. See you tomorrow."

He hung up. That was how it started.

CHAPTER 2

I WAS ALONE in my office off of Shelly Minck's dental chamber of mayhem. I had left the lights on and the doors open for Grant. There wasn't much going on in the Farraday on New Year's Day. I had taken the straining elevator up the five flights, listening to its echo below. The building lights weren't on, but there was enough light coming through the skylights in the ceiling to cast impressive late morning shadows.

The Farraday was, thanks to Jeremy Butler, always clean and smelling of Lysol, one of my favorite scents. The turn-of-the-century ironwork of the railings, stairwell, and painfully slow elevator created dark, intricate patterns that kaleidoscoped as I moved upward.

Jeremy and his family lived in converted offices on the seventh floor of the Farraday. It wasn't that they couldn't afford more. Jeremy had property on both sides of the hills: two one-story courtyard apartments, a small office building in North Hollywood, and others he didn't talk about much.

I had pushed open the doors of the elevator, listening first to the creaking echo and then to my footsteps as I moved toward my office. I heard something and looked down over the railing.

"Toby?" came a voice from below.

"Jeremy?" I answered. Our voices echoed.

Below me, Jeremy Butler came out of the shadows. He carried a familiar mop and bucket.

Jeremy and his wife, Alice, had left Mrs. Plaut's party early, just minutes after midnight. Jeremy had carried their sleeping two-year-old, Natasha, a cherubic kid with dark curly ringlets who looked nothing like either of her parents.

"They got in," Jeremy called.

I knew who "they" were—the homeless, the wandering alcoholics, the people who cruised Main and Hoover occasionally asking for a handout, usually on their way to or from one of the small parks near downtown.

"How bad?" I asked.

"Not too bad," Jeremy said.

He was big enough and strong enough even at the age of sixty-one to heave a dozen intruders into the New Year with one hand. But that wasn't Jeremy.

"We endure," he said, looking around so that I saw the sun glinting off the top of his bald head. "Your client will be here soon?"

I had told Jeremy the night before that I had a client coming and had asked him to leave the front door open.

"Soon," I said.

"After Alice and Natasha went to bed this morning, I wrote a new poem."

"I'd like to hear it," I said.

"I'll be up in a few minutes," he said before I could ask him to wait until Cary Grant had come and gone. But when the muse hit

Jeremy, he wanted to share his creations with Alice and me. My knowledge and appreciation of poetry was slender, but I was a good audience. A significant part of my business was knowing how to be a good audience.

I turned and went to the pebbled glass door on which was lettered in gold: "Sheldon Minck, D.D.S., S.V.U., L.U., Dentist." In smaller letters below this was "Toby Peters, Confidential Investigations." The "Confidential Investigations" had been Violet Gonsenelli's idea.

"Class," she said. "Distinguishes you from the crowd."

I went into the small waiting-reception room, turned on the lights, and went into Shelly's office. When I hit the switch there, I was greeted by a surprise. The room, tools, dental chair, and metal table were sparkling clean. There were no dirty dishes and discarded instruments of torment piled in the sink against the wall. The garbage can was empty, not a single two-day-old wad of bloody cotton.

This should have been a warning. Instead I felt a tinge of relief. Cary Grant wouldn't be walking into the Spanish Inquisitor's dungeon.

My office was open. I went to the window, raised it, then turned on the fan on my desk and sat. I didn't bother to look at my father's watch. I had a wind-up clock on my desk, but it had run down and I liked it better that way. It wasn't that I didn't want to know the time. What I didn't want was to listen to each second of time ticking away. I preferred to check other people's clocks and watches.

I knew it was about eleven o'clock. I had looked at the clock in the window of Vitterman's jewelry store on Hoover after I had parked the Crosley.

The New Year's party had been less than riotous. My sister-in-law, Ruth, had been too sick to come. She had been getting worse over the last few months. So, my brother, Phil, hadn't shown up. Shelly had come alone, still pining for his wife, Mildred, who had left him, taking everything that wasn't welded to the floor. Actually, she had taken very little. Shelly had been booted out of their house. In his place there was a gaffer from RKO. The gaffer was big, brawny, and ugly. Mildred was no prize in looks or personality either. Yet Shelly still longed for her and the bad old days. Shelly had gotten mildly drunk on Mrs. Plaut's special brew of unidentified alcohol-and-fruit punch.

Gunther had drunk one cup of the brew and eaten one of Mrs. P's famous Zanzibar cookies made with coffee, flour, sugar, and whatever nuts or pieces of fruit might be handy. Niece Emma Simcox and tenant Ben Bidwell were there. Bidwell and Emma had danced to Mrs. Plaut's records of Gene Austin, Russ Colombo, and Bing Crosby. Surprisingly, for a man with only one arm, Bidwell was a damn good dancer, inventive.

Anita and I had sat together, talking about high school, past spouses, her daughter, the war, and which movie we were going to see on Thursday, her day off. The choice was hers. She said she wanted to see *Thank Your Lucky Stars*, the war-effort musical with Humphrey Bogart, Eddie Cantor, Bette Davis, Errol Flynn, Olivia deHavilland, Ida Lupino, Dennis Morgan, and John Garfield. I told her Davis and Flynn had both been clients of mine. She was impressed.

"You look a lot like John Garfield," she said, "except for the nose." Meaning Garfield had one and mine had been smashed pug flat.

"Thanks," I said.

We danced. A few years ago I had been given a few lessons by Fred Astaire, and, while I still wouldn't make it to the back-up chorus, I now knew how to find the beat and look respectable on the floor. Anita had a good time.

At ten minutes to midnight, Juanita had risen, clapped her hands, and silenced the gathering by turning off Rudy Vallee in mid-"Goodnight, Sweetheart."

Juanita was dressed sedately, at least for her. That meant fewer spangles and bangles, a black skirt, and a billowing blouse with a rainbow of colored dots. She announced in her distinct Bronx accent that it was now 1944.

Then she added, "For some of you I see things in the new year. For some. . . ." She looked at Shelly, who was gazing pitifully into his cup of red liquid, "I see nothing."

"One or two things for each of the rest of you," she said.

Juanita looked at Jeremy, Alice, and Natasha and said, "The child will be a scholar. I see her writing books. I don't know what-the-hell kind."

Then she turned to Gunther, "Love comes."

To Mrs. Plaut, she said cryptically, "It will be over soon."

Mrs. Plaut nodded in understanding.

To Emma Simcox, she said, "He will be back sooner than you expect."

Bidwell was next. Juanita shook her head and said, "It's not gonna happen, but you're gonna make a ton of money."

It was Anita's turn.

"She'll break your heart."

And then to me she said with a sigh, "You won't fall. Listen to the man above. He'll save you."

As usual, Juanita's insights into the future meant nothing to me, though she had obviously touched a note with Mrs. Plaut and her niece, Emma.

"That's it," Mrs. Plaut suddenly announced. "It's twelve thirty-seven."

Mrs. Plaut blessed us all, told me to take Miss Anita home, and ordered her other boarders to hit their rooms.

"Tomorrow is here," she announced.

Everyone left dutifully except Shelly, who wanted to talk about the Rose Bowl. Washington was the big favorite. He was rooting for USC. Washington had gone through the season undefeated. I doubted that Shelly knew that. In fact, I was sure he knew just about nothing about college football or any other sport. He just didn't want to go to the hotel room he'd been living in since Mildred had booted him out.

"Time to go, Shel," I had said, noticing that he must have had more than a few cups of Mrs. Plaut's punch.

"Going to clean up the office," he said, as Anita and I helped him up. "New year. Resolution. Right now. Today, before I change my mind. Fresh start."

"Great idea," I said. "We'll drive you home."

"Going to the office," he had insisted, his thick glasses slipping precariously down his nose, his breath smelling of cheap cigars and Mrs. Plaut's punch.

Mrs. Plaut allowed no smoking in her boardinghouse. This had been a distinct hardship for Shelly, who was seldom without a thick cigar, even when he was working on a patient.

"I shall drive the doctor home," Gunther announced.

Shelly smiled.

"Can't reach the pedals of my car," he said. "Can't see over the wheel."

"We will take my car," Gunther had said.

Gunther's car had a built-up seat and special blocks on the gas and brake pedals.

"Take your key, Mr. Gunther," Mrs. Plaut, said starting to clean up with Emma's help. "You, too, Mr. Peelers."

Happy New Year greetings were exchanged for about the fifth time before our quartet went out into the cool Los Angeles night. Anita and I helped Shelly to Gunther's car and tucked him into the backseat.

I didn't ask Gunther how he was going to get Shelly into his hotel room. Gunther was strong for a little man, and resourceful.

After I took Anita to her apartment and gave her a kiss at the door, I told her I'd try to stop by the drugstore on Monday.

Then I had gone back to Mrs. Plaut's and made my way to my room and my mattress.

That was then. This was now. Now I sat waiting for Cary Grant, coming to the conclusion that, as drunk as Shelly was, he must have convinced Gunther to bring him to the office. There he had made good on his New Year's resolution and spent the rest of the night cleaning the office.

A disturbing thought. Shelly might still be lurking somewhere in the Farraday. Maybe he had searched out one of the other New Year's Day workers, probably Dave Halbermeyer, the child photographer, or Sidney Wyland of Wyland and Associates, Film and Theatrical Agents. There were no Associates. Sidney Wyland was a one-man operation representing bit-player clients—and not many of those.

I heard the door to the reception room open and got up to open my door. Jeremy was moving across the room, his eyes taking in the office which now looked as if a patient might expect reasonably sanitary treatment. That would be a potentially fatal mistake.

"You have a few minutes?" Jeremy asked as I moved back into my office and he filled the doorway. My office was a tight fit for Jeremy.

"Sure," I said. "Have a seat."

"I'll stand," he said, reaching into his pocket.

He wore dark slacks, a blue long-sleeved pullover shirt, and a serious look—his poetry look. He launched into it.

> When camels climb the stairs on padded feet,
> and magma from a remote eruption rushes uphill,

the world has not gone mad with heat,
the God or Gods have not become suddenly ill.
It is the nature of nature that anything can be.
It is the lesson of the texts from Scripture to Koran.
There for all who look to clearly see,
there to tell us that there really is no plan.
The key to peace is our ability to accept
that elephants might fly, that ants might sing,
that there is no foundation except
that one never knows what the next moment may bring.
And in that knowledge we can be made free.
We are bound only by what we do and wish to be.

"I like the Dumbo reference," I said, knowing I had to say something.

"It needed humor," Jeremy said humorlessly, tucking the poem away.

"Humor's a good thing," I agreed.

"You think it's ready for publication? Alice does."

"It's ready," I said. "Deep."

"It's what I believe," he said.

"I can see that."

"Thank you, Toby," he said turning. "Dr. Minck's office is a good example of the essence of my poem."

"I was just thinking that," I said as Jeremy departed, closing my door behind him.

It opened almost immediately and I thought Jeremy had returned, but it was Cary Grant.

He was wearing khaki slacks, a white shirt, and a lightweight striped sports jacket. No tie.

"You must be Toby Peters," he said, reaching over the desk with his hand out. He gave me a small smile showing even white teeth. He looked genuinely glad to meet me, though I'd done nothing yet to earn his goodwill or money.

We shook. His grip was firm.

"Do you mind if I sit?" he asked, looking around the small office.

"Seems like a good idea."

"Cozy," he said, straightening his pants and sitting with his legs crossed. His eyes turned to the painting on the wall.

"Dalí," he said. "Early. I'm impressed."

He put on his glasses and examined it more closely.

"An original," he said with respect.

He was tan, and his dark hair lay neatly in place. I knew a few things about him that everyone knew. I knew he was married to Barbara Hutton, the Woolworth heiress, whom he never called 'Babs.' I knew he had been married a couple of times before, including to Virginia Cherrill who'd played the blind girl in Charlie Chaplin's *City Lights*. I knew his movies. Anita and I had seen his latest, *Destination Tokyo*, two weeks ago.

"Sorry to get you up so early on New Year's Day," he said, in that accent that was so easy to imitate and difficult to perfect. "But, believe me, it is important."

"I went to bed early," I said.

"So did I," he said. "Barbara threw one of her parties. I'm all right with parties in moderation and spaced well apart. In fact, I like them when they're with close friends and very small."

"Me too," I said.

He bit his lower lip and looked down at his hands for a moment.

"I'm avoiding the reason for my coming," he said.

"Take your time."

He nodded.

"As I told you on the phone, a friend recommended you," he

said after a long pause. "Peter Lorre. He told me about you last year when we were doing *Arsenic and Old Lace*."

"Funny movie," I said.

"Yes, but I wasn't happy with it. Too much, too broad. It should have been Jimmy Stewart instead of me. I told Capra but . . . I'm avoiding again. I'll get to it. Peter said you could be trusted."

"Says 'Confidential Investigations' right on my door."

"Yes, but, no offense, there are a lot of things on doors and cards and in letters and conversation that bear little resemblance to reality."

"Your choice," I said. "You want references?"

"I've checked your references with a few people you've worked for. They said you could be trusted. Well, I'm going to trust you. I'd like to hire you for a job. Only a few hours. Tonight."

"Don't you want to know my fee?"

"I'm sure you'll be reasonable," he said.

We sat silently for few seconds while he considered how to tell me.

"I should have rehearsed this," he finally said, "but here goes. Do you have a gun?"

"Yes," I said. "A thirty-eight."

I didn't tell him that it rested in the locked glove compartment of my Crosley and that I seldom touched it. I was a lousy shot. When I had been a cop in Burbank, I almost shot my own partner in the only shoot-out I've ever been in. I had shot one person with that .38 since I'd become a private detective, and that had been up close and not what I had planned. The gun had also been used once to shoot me. I shared none of this with Grant, just sat there trying to look tough, competent, and confident.

"Good," said Grant. "I don't think this is going to be dangerous but . . ."

"But . . . ," I picked up.

He sighed.

"I'm going to give you a small bag," he said, "and tell you a place to take it tonight. You'll meet someone who will give you something. You take it, give him the bag, and meet me somewhere."

"That's it?"

"That's it," he said.

"Mind some questions?"

"Probably," he said, "but it makes sense that you'd have them. Go ahead."

"Why don't you just make this exchange yourself?"

"The person or people I'm dealing with said I shouldn't."

"And it might be dangerous?" I asked.

"It shouldn't be," he said. "You give them the bag. You get the package. Do you want to know what's in the bag and the package?"

"I'm curious," I said.

"Money will be in the bag, Mr. Peters," he said, leaning forward. "Quite a lot of money. And the package will contain certain documents. Compromising documents."

I sat silently.

"No," he said. "I'm not being blackmailed over some crime or sexual indiscretion. It's more important than that. That's all I can tell you except that nothing illegal is going on. It's a simple transaction. I'm paying for something, and I expect to get what I pay for. I'm afraid that's all I can tell you."

"All you're willing to tell me."

"All I'm willing to tell you," he agreed. "So, have I hired a confidential investigator?"

"Since this is a one-night rush job, let's just say two hundred dollars, flat fee."

Grant pursed his lips.

"Your price has gone up," he said with a smile.

"I'm going into this in the dark with a bag full of money and people you don't trust."

"Point taken," he said, reaching into his jacket and removing his wallet. "I assume you won't mind cash."

"I won't mind cash. I'll give you a receipt."

"No receipt, no written bills," he said. "No record of this."

"Suit yourself," I said as he handed over four fifty-dollar bills.

I was suddenly wealthy. I owed No-Neck Arnie twenty-seven dollars. I'd stop by his shop and pay him if he was in. It was only two blocks from the Farraday.

"I live in Pacific Palisades," he said. "I'd meet you there, but it might be a bit awkward. The place is full of Barbara's assistants, butlers, and maids. My wife and I . . . never mind. There's a bar in Santa Monica, a little place on the beach called Wally's."

"I've seen it," I said.

"The owner's a friend of mine. Can you be there at ten tonight? I'll give you the bag and tell you what to do next when you get there."

"I'll be there at ten," I said.

"Fine," Grant said, standing and holding out his hand again. We shook for the second time. "I'm counting on you, Peters."

"I'll walk down with you," I said.

We went into Shelly's office and were greeted by the sight of Sheldon Minck slouched down in his dental chair, his clothes as messy as the room was clean. He needed a shave. He needed a bath. He needed serious fumigation and a fresh cigar. His glasses were on his forehead.

"I did it, Toby," he said, looking around the office. "A new beginning."

"You did a great job, Shel," I said.

Shelly squinted in our direction, fumbled for his glasses, and managed to drop them down on his nose, although there was a serious tilt to the left.

"I know you," Shelly said, looking at Grant.

My new client looked at me.

"This is Dr. Minck," I said. "This is his office. He's a dentist. He's hungover."

"Why don't you add that my wife left me?" Shelly said checking what was left of his cigar and searching his pockets for a match. "Then you'd have my whole life story. Four sentences. That's it."

"Pleasure to meet you, Dr. Minck," Grant said.

"Got it," Shelly said, leaning forward but not getting out of the chair. "George Kaplan, Jefferson High. You were a few years after me. You did imitations for the annual Maskers Night. You're doing someone now."

"I'm not George Kaplan," Grant said.

Shelly looked again.

"We've really got to get going, Shel," I said, moving toward the door.

"If you're not Kaplan, you look a hell of a lot like him," Shelly said suspiciously.

"It's my curse," said Grant. "People are frequently confusing us. I've sent apologies to Kaplan a number of times, but he doesn't respond."

"Sounds like Kaplan," said Shelly. "I mean it sounds like Kaplan not to answer. Not that you sound like Kaplan. You sound like the actor. David Niven. But you don't look like him."

"I'll be back in a few seconds, Shel," I said, my hand on the doorknob.

"I'm alone, Toby," he said. "No patients. No Mildred. No friends. Well, not many friends."

"It's a sad story, Shel," I said, opening the door.

"It was a pleasure meeting you, Dr. Minck," Grant said, following me out. Shelly didn't answer.

In the hall, Grant asked, "Is he always like that?"

"He's having a good day," I said. "You should see him when he's depressed."

"I think I'll forgo that pleasure."

"Stairs or elevator?" I asked.

"I took the elevator up," said Grant, moving briskly toward the stairs. "I don't really have the time to take it down."

So I stood at the railing, watching him as he moved quickly down the stairs.

CHAPTER 3

SHELLY WAS STILL slumped in his dental chair when I went past him heading back to my office. He looked up and shook his head.

"How much can one man take?" he said with a massive sigh.

A hell of a lot more than you're dealing with, Sheldon, I thought. But aloud I said, "You'll make it, Shel. You're a resourceful human being."

"I am, aren't I?" he asked, looking up.

"That's something I've always admired about you," I said, my hand now on the knob of my office door.

There really wasn't much I admired about Shelly, and certainly not his resourcefulness. My experience with him was that whenever he tried to fall back on his instincts or intellect, he took a dive instead.

I went into my office and sat behind my desk. It wasn't noon yet. I had most of the day to go before I had to meet Grant at Wally's. I opened the center drawer in my desk and pulled out the sheet of paper Violet had handed me two days earlier. Then I took the black-and-white composition book from the bottom right-hand drawer and placed it in front of me.

The book contained my notes on jobs I still had open or on ones not completed either to the client's satisfaction or my own. I opened the book. There wasn't much in it. I wasn't much for details. I flipped through, spotting names written in pencil.

Wayne Bonidavente. Wayne owned a bar in Van Nuys. Someone had been dipping into the cash drawer. He had been losing about thirty dollars a day. Only Wayne, his wife, Ellie, and his brother, Warren, tended bar and used the cash drawer. I had sat there for a week, drinking beer very slowly and listening to unhappy wives and husbands tell me their tales.

I was an easy target, sitting alone, nursing the hell out of a beer night after night. Every approach was the same. The man or woman came up to me, drink in hand, smiling and saying, "Mind if I join you?" Meaning, I'm lonely as hell and I want to tell someone my story and I'm willing to listen to yours and give you advice if you'll listen to mine but I wouldn't mind it much if I didn't have to listen to yours.

I'd spent a week in Wayne's bar listening to stories and watching Ellie and Warren on their shifts. Never saw them pocketing a dime. I did hear a few good stories, though.

Wayne reported each day that a different amount was missing. What was being rung up on the cash register simply didn't match what was in the drawer when he counted the take.

I liked Ellie, who had thin, stringy hair, and an understanding smile. And I liked brother Warren, who was pushing late middle age with thin white hair, a thin mustache, and a little pot belly. He liked his little Cuban cigars and thought he looked like Gilbert Roland.

"Which one?" asked Wayne, about fifty, his hair too dark and definitely dyed.

When he asked me the question, I knew, but I couldn't tell him. He wouldn't believe me. I had to say that it was a mystery I couldn't solve, that I didn't believe either his wife or brother was pocketing the money.

What I didn't tell him was that I had, after six nights, and just before Ellie was about to leave on her two-to-ten shift, asked Wayne's wife and brother if I could talk to them.

They weren't busy yet although there were some regulars I recognized, a few of whom had nodded at me. We talked at the bar, the two of them next to each other, leaning forward.

"I'm a private detective," I said. "Wayne hired me. Someone's dipping into the cash register every night. The profits are going. If it doesn't stop, this place will fold. So it stops tonight. Now. We understand each other?"

Ellie and Warren looked at each other, and Warren nodded to her.

"Wayne is taking it," she said. "He pockets cash. I've seen him."

"Then why did he hire me?"

"He doesn't know he's doing it," said Warren. "At least, I don't think he does. He gets this kind of zombie look when he does it."

"I don't get it," I said.

"There's something wrong inside Wayne's brain," said Ellie.

"Happened to our old man too," Warren added. "When the old man died, they found a thing on his brain. We think maybe Wayne's got it too. We've tried to get him to see a doctor about it. He says there's nothing wrong with him."

"What does he do with the money?"

Warren shrugged.

"Beats me. Maybe he's putting it in a box somewhere. Maybe he throws it away."

"He's not buying anything with it," Ellie said.

"Got any suggestions? We're listening," Warren said.

I had none, so I told Wayne I couldn't figure it out and offered to return the money he had already paid me.

Wayne's case was in my composition book. I sometimes wondered what had happened to the three of them. My last meeting with Wayne had been about four years ago. I kept thinking I would call the bar sometime and ask Ellie or Warren how Wayne was doing, but I could never bring myself to do it. I just kept the case open in my book.

Then there were the Cherik brothers. They were bulky, almost twins who were arrested for nearly beating to death a hot dog vendor in Pershing Square. The vendor identified them. They had records, nothing big, and made what looked like an honest or semi-honest living taking small bets on everything. The hot dog guy was one of their customers. They hired me and swore they hadn't done it. I believed them.

For four days I looked for two guys who might resemble the Cheriks. I talked to the hot dog vendor. He was certain. He had no reason to lie. I talked to the Cheriks again and still believed them. They got sent behind bars for six months and dished out a fine that wiped them out.

I still believe them. In my book, I had penciled in the last thing Tony Cherik had said to me, "Sometimes you pay for something you didn't do to balance it out with stuff you did do, you know? So maybe we do some time and that wipes us clean for other stuff."

The Cheriks were not philosopher material, but I liked their attitude. They wouldn't take back the money they had paid me up front. The Cherik case was still open.

Then there's the one I promised not to talk about. All I can say is that the client was Greta Garbo. That one had a conclusion. It just wasn't one she wanted to talk about, and I had promised never to say anything about it. I can, however, say that I remember one thing she told me.

"I don't really like being alone," she had said. "I'm just very particular about whom I am willing to spend my time with."

There were more such cases. Eleven altogether. But I had the feeling that I might be about to get the list down to ten because of the note Violet had given me.

I looked at the entry in my book. There was a photograph

tucked along the binding. It was a picture of a cat looking right at the camera. A fat cat. I had been told the cat was silver with black streaks. I had been told that his name was Granger. I didn't have to be told by his owner, Louise Antolini, that Granger had a hunk of his left ear missing.

"He went out one night and came back like that," Mrs. Antolini had explained. "You have a pet?"

"No," I said.

My brother and I had had the German shepherd, Kaiser Wilhelm, when I was a kid. I don't remember much about him other than that he seemed to like me and not my brother, especially after Phil came back from the war they now called World War I. A cat named Dash had sort of started living with me about the time Louise Antolini lost track of Granger, but Dash wasn't a pet. He had saved my life once. I owed him. I left my window open at Mrs. Plaut's, and Dash came and went when he felt like it. I fed him. Sometimes he slept on the small couch in my room. I always slept on a thin mattress on the floor. Bad back. Long story.

The note from Violet. I had failed to find Granger, and Louise Antolini, as regular as the seasons, sent me letters demanding to know what progress I was making. She had paid me a total of seventy-five dollars. I had used all of it and more to run small ads once a week in the *Times*. The ads read: "Missing one-eared cat. Reward." I added my phone number. Once in a while I got a call. I never had to go out and look at the discovered cats or ask the finders to bring them to me for the reward. I had a series of questions about the cat for each caller. All had failed to answer the questions, but the one on Violet's message held promise. It read:

> CALL SAMUEL STINOVENOV IN THE ACUTE UNIT AT COUNTY HOSPITAL. HE'S GOT A GRAY CAT WITH BLACK STRIPES AND A MISSING LEFT EAR. SAYS YOU'D KNOW.

Violet had taken no phone number. None had been given. I checked the greater L.A. phone book. No Stinovenov.

I called the hospital and asked for the Acute Unit.

"Samuel Stinovenov," I said to the woman who answered the phone.

"He's off today," she said.

"I'm his brother Julian," I said. "I'm in town for one day. Can you give me his phone number?"

"Brother?" the woman asked.

"Julian," I repeated.

She put her hand over the receiver, but I could hear her muffled voice say to someone, "You know Sam has a brother?"

I didn't hear the answer, but she came back on and said, "I'm looking."

She hummed while she looked, came back quickly, and said, "You don't have an accent."

"I've worked on it," I said.

"Say something in Russian."

"Huh?"

"You're Russian," she said. "Say something."

"*Vosnushev leskronik menchovenola*," I said.

"What does that mean?"

"It means 'you have a very melodic voice,'" I said, relieved that she knew no Russian.

She gave me the number. A detective was at work here. I dialed the number. It rang five times and a man with a Russian accent answered.

"Hello."

"Samuel Stinovenov?"

"Yes."

"I'm calling about the cat."

"How much?"

"The reward?" I asked.

"Yes, how much?"

"Thirty dollars," I said, hoping I could get the money back from Louise Antolini.

"Where you want me to bring cat?"

"Some questions first," I said.

I didn't ask him to call the cat Granger and see if he came running. Cats answer or don't answer, depending on their mood. I asked him how old he thought the cat was. He said he thought it was not a young cat. I asked him where he lived. It was near the hospital, just off of State Street. I said I'd be right over.

"With cash money," he said.

"With cash money," I agreed and hung up, pocketing the photograph of Granger.

Shelly was still in the dental chair. He was eating an apple and talking to himself. I couldn't hear what he was saying. I didn't say good-bye.

My car was parked right in front of the Farraday Building. Normally, it was so crowded on Hoover and on Main I parked two blocks away at No-Neck Arnie's. But this was New Year's Day and a Saturday, to boot. So I had had my choice of spots.

I drove to Arnie's. His rusting metal garage doors were open. I drove through them and stopped behind a blue Oldsmobile. Arnie, dressed in his grease-stained gray overalls, was looking into the yawning car. He pulled his head out from under the hood and turned to look at me when I got out of the Crosley.

"I wasn't sure you'd be in today," I said, joining him next to the Olds.

It wasn't true that Arnie had no neck. But it was close. Arnie was short, compact, and looked a little like Winston Churchill. Arnie had more hair and no accent.

"Couldn't stay home," he said. "I was too excited."

Arnie didn't look excited. He looked sad, but Arnie always looked sad.

"What?"

"Arnie Junior's coming home," he said. "He called from a hospital in Hawaii. Wounded again. Shrapnel in the leg. He says he'll be fine. They're sending him home."

"That's great," I said.

"It's great," he agreed. "Wife's goin' all around telling her sisters, friends. Me, I just felt like coming in here and taking another crack at this thing."

He looked inside near the engine.

"What's the problem?"

"Damn automatic transmission," he said. "Never works right. Clunks when it changes gear. G.M. says they're got the problems licked and are going to try it on the Buick after the war. Mistake. Never catch on. What's so damn hard about shifting gears?"

"Nothing," I said.

"Nothing," he agreed.

I took out my wallet and held out the money I owed him. He wiped his hand on his overalls and took the cash.

"Want a Pepsi?" he asked, knowing my drink of choice.

He pocketed the money without putting it in his wallet.

"No time," I said. "Got to see a guy with a cat."

"How's she running?" he asked as I walked back to my car.

"Like a refrigerator," I said.

An hour later, after picking up Granger and making a phone call from Stinovenov's two-room apartment, I was in front of Louise Antolini's front door in Westwood.

She opened the door before I knocked and took the cat from my arms, which was fine with me since Granger had scratched me as soon as he saw the house. I got the feeling he preferred the open road. I also got the feeling he would be back on it again as soon as he could escape the smothering kisses smacking against his furry face.

"Granger, Granger, Granger. No longer a stranger," she said, looking at me triumphantly while holding the cat tightly against her more than ample breasts. "I've been waiting to say that for more than two years. Is he all right?"

Till he saw your house, I thought, but said, "Fine. I had to pay a thirty-dollar reward to the guy who found him."

"People shouldn't take money for returning other people's missing pets," she said, clutching the meowing cat. The noise didn't seem to be a result of pleasure but of Granger's desire to escape. Maybe I was seeing more than was there. I knew I was hearing what I didn't want to hear.

"They shouldn't," I agreed. "But they do."

"I'm not paying," she said. "For all I know, whoever is demanding this ransom took Granger in the first place."

"And kept him for two years?" I asked. "He saw my ad in the paper, spotted Granger hanging around the hospital."

"Hospital?"

"County. The guy who found your cat is a nurse."

"A man is a nurse?" she asked, bestowing further kisses on the cat, whose eyes were now closed.

"It happens. He's Russian. I paid him thirty dollars."

"You weren't authorized to do that," she said.

"I . . . ," I began. But before I could finish she had closed the door.

Another job completed by Toby Peters, Confidential Investigator.

"Happy New Year," I told the closed door.

To cheer myself up I drove to Hancock Park, parked on the street with no problem, and went through the entrance at Wilshire and Curson. I headed right for the La Brea Tar Pits near the center of the park. The pits are bogs with subterranean oil and tar bubbling slowly to the surface. A pool of water camouflages the sticky sludge that had been a trap for unwary animals gathering there thousands of years earlier to drink from what they thought was a quiet pool. Skeletal remains of saber-toothed tigers, Imperial elephants, woolly mammoths, giant sloths, condors, Great American lions, and even a specimen of the only American peacock had been found and removed from the pits. Birds of prey and carrion-eaters had fed on these doomed, sinking animals and sometimes they, too, had been caught in the bog.

On days like today, the pits suggested that Los Angeles had not changed much since the days of the dinosaurs.

I stood there alone, watching a black bubble as it expanded into a surface balloon. A woman with two children came up and stood a few feet away. She had a book in her hand. We all looked at the pit, waiting.

And then the bubble burst.

I still had most of the day till I had to meet Grant at Wally's. I didn't feel like going back to the Farraday, and I definitely didn't want to go back to Mrs. Plaut's.

I left the car parked where it was, picked up a copy of the *L. A. Times* from a hotel lobby, and walked two blocks to J & W's Downtown Restaurant. I arrived a little after the lunch crowd, had there been one on New Year's Day. I got a table near the kitchen, ordered a tuna on white, fries and coffee, and looked at the paper.

Twenty minutes later and eighty cents lighter, I knew that Japanese girls were now wearing slacks or *mompei* instead of kimonos; was reminded that USC was going to play undefeated Washington in the Rose Bowl in a few hours; that Alley Oop, stone ax in hand, was lost in time; that Scorchy Smith was being transfered to combat duty; that the Red Army, under Ukrainian General Nikolai Vatotin, was within twenty-seven miles of the Polish border; and that the Royal Air Force had bombed Berlin for the ninth straight day.

I headed for Santa Monica in light traffic. I spent the rest of the afternoon sitting on the beach, looking at girls and watching the waves come in. I read the paper. For part of the time, I kept an eye on a fat couple in their fifties who were taking turns looking at the Pacific through a pair of binoculars. I figured they were looking for a Jap sub so they could be the first to call in the sighting to Civil Defense and get their picture in the paper.

I put my folded newspaper on the sand and lay back to look at the clouds and wait for the sunset. I fell asleep and woke up to the sound of laughter. A young couple was about thirty yards away. She laughed. He kissed her. I sat up, wondering what time it was. I had missed the sunset. It was dark. The beach was almost empty and the air had a chill.

Carefully, hoping my back would be all right, I sat up. No problem. Back in the Crosley, I turned on the radio. The news ended, so I knew it was a quarter to ten. I checked my .38 in the glove compartment and then drove the mile to Wally's.

CHAPTER

WALLY'S WAS AT the base of the hills, a gas station on one side and a souvenir shop on the other. The gas station and the shop were closed. There were six cars in front of Wally's. I tried to figure out which one was Grant's, if he had even arrived yet. All the cars looked like money. I pulled my Crosley into a spot next to a big fat Chrysler.

Wally's was surprisingly long, and darkly amber lit. The bar ran along the left. There were small booths on the right and space down the middle heading toward the back, where two doors were clearly marked for ladies and gentlemen. Between the two doors was a pay phone mounted on the wall.

There were five people at the bar talking, a few couples in the booths. Nobody was young. All were dressed casually, but with class, except the guy behind the bar in an apron. He looked a little like Wallace Beery. He looked my way and said, "You Peters?"

"Yeah."

He nodded toward the rear of the place and I headed back.

There was a single high-backed wooden booth at the rear. There was no one on the side facing the bar. Grant sat with his back to the bar on the other side, wearing a black knit turtle-neck shirt under a gray sports jacket.

"Peters," he said. "You're right on time."

I sat across from him. He had a drink in front of him.

"Hungry?" he asked. "Wally makes a good spiced chicken sandwich on a Kaiser roll."

"Sure," I said.

Grant raised his hand over the top of the booth. The bartender came over to the table.

"A chicken sandwich for my friend," he said and turned to me. "What're you drinking?"

"Pepsi."

Wally nodded and disappeared.

"We're alone and unobserved," he said. "Now I can admit that I'm an aesthetic sham."

I looked at him.

"Gilbert and Sullivan," he said. "The only problem with this booth is that I have to look at the doors to the restrooms if there's no one across from me."

He reached down to the seat next to him and came up with a thick leather pouch about the size of a book. He pushed it toward me.

"I can't tell you very much," he said, "but I can tell you there's five thousand dollars in that bag."

I looked at the bag.

"You're still thinking blackmail. No," he said. "Blackmail's been tried on me. A few years ago a man who had been fired from RKO publicity tried to get money out of me. He said he had photos and proof that Randolph Scott and I were lovers."

He looked at me for a reaction. There was a small familiar smile on his face.

"He was wrong," Grant said. "My wives and a small number of young ladies could have told him that. Scotty and I shared a place for a few years. We had lots of visitors, mostly ladies. The would-be blackmailer said it didn't matter if it was true or not. He had pictures of me and Scotty in our bathing suits, arms around each other's shoulders. He had a picture of me in a woman's robe with fluffy sleeves. I told him I'd get back to him."

Grant took a sip of his drink, his eyes on me.

"Want to know what I did?"

"Ordered copies of the pictures?" I asked.

"The picture of me in the woman's robe was a still from *Bringing up Baby*."

"The one where you have to put on Katharine Hepburn's robe when you get wet and when someone sees you and asks what you're doing, you say, 'I've suddenly gone gay.'"

"A fan," Grant said with a laugh and shook his head. "I told the police," he said. "They asked me if I wanted to press charges. I told them I'd be happy if the man with the pictures just went away. That was the last I heard from him."

"No blackmail," I said.

"No blackmail," he repeated. "No dark personal secrets. I'm now simply paying a man for some information I need."

I could have asked why the guy with the information didn't just come to Wally's, pick up his pouch, and give Grant his information, but I had already parted with a good chunk of the actor's money to return a cat to a purgatory of smothering love.

"You give him the bag," he said. "He gives you an envelope."

"That's why you said I should bring a gun?"

Grant pursed his lips and tapped the tips of the fingers of both hands against each other for a few seconds.

"I don't know the man. Never met him. That's the way he wants to keep it. I think I did recognize his voice when he called. I'm not sure from where. He gave me enough information to convince me that what he was selling was genuine and worth the price."

Drugs, I thought.

"Not drugs," Grant said, reading my easily readable face. "But something that could get him in serious trouble if certain people knew he was selling it to me."

"Now I understand," I said.

"No, you don't. And I don't think you want to. There shouldn't be any trouble. He wants the money. I want the envelope. Questions?"

"Where do I deliver?" I asked as Wally finally returned with my Pepsi.

He looked at Grant to see if he wanted a refill on his drink. Grant shook his head "no." When Wally had gone, Grant said, "I don't know. He's going to phone here and tell me where he wants it delivered."

"And he doesn't want you to deliver it?"

"No. I think he's afraid I'll recognize him even if he's wearing something to cover his face."

"So we wait, have a few drinks."

"And Wally's famous chicken sandwich."

"I can live with that," I said.

The radio at the bar played dance band music I didn't recognize and Grant kept looking at his watch. At one point he wrote a phone number on a napkin and handed it to me. I put it in my pocket. Then the pay phone rang. Grant looked at his watch, got up, and moved to the phone.

I took the small notebook from my pocket, along with one of two sharpened pencils. I got up and moved to Grant's side. He covered his left ear with his hand to block out the noise of the dance band and the customers at the bar.

"Yes," Grant said. "His name is . . . all right, you don't need his name. Describe him? He's about five-nine. . . ."

I nodded in agreement. It was close enough.

"Slightly stocky, dark hair with some gray," Grant went on. "Face like a boxer. Flat nose. He's wearing dark slacks, a white shirt, and a blue zipper jacket . . . I don't know."

Grant turned to me, covered the receiver with his hand and looked at me.

"He wants to know if you're carrying a gun."

I reached into the pocket of my jacket and pulled the handle of my .38 high enough for Grant to see.

"He is carrying a gun," Grant said. "And he's going to have it on him. He's a former policeman, an expert shot."

Grant listened and nodded and then said aloud looking at me, "Madman Dumar's on San Vicente just south of Wilshire."

I nodded. I knew Madman Dumar's Autos. He ran ads on KFWB radio. Dumar talked fast and loud and promised that every car he sold was sure to please at a price you couldn't afford to pass up. "I'm crazy," Dumar said ten or fifteen times a day on 950 on my radio dial. "Come down and see how crazy I can be." Dumar wasn't crazy enough to be open after ten on New Year's Day.

"Phone booth at the north end of the lot," Grant repeated for my benefit. "Eleven-fifteen. He'll be there."

Grant hung up the phone.

"What time is it?" I asked.

Grant looked at the watch on my wrist.

"It doesn't work," I said. "It was my father's. Tells its own time." Grant lifted an eyebrow.

"It's twenty minutes to eleven," he said. "I'll call you in the morning to be sure it went all right. If something goes wrong, call me at the number I gave you, but only if something goes wrong. Good luck. And be careful."

"I will," I said. "What did he say when you told him I had a gun?"

Grant hesitated, and then he said, "He hoped it was a big one and that you knew how to use it."

We shook hands. Grant stood watching as I walked back through Wally's and out the door. It took me nearly half an hour to get to Madman Dumar's. When I got there, I parked right next to the phone booth and got out. There wasn't much traffic, but there were some cars going in both directions.

Madman Dumar's lot was filled with cars that had signs with prices on their windshields. The prices were in bright red on big white cards. There was a billboard above the lot with a caricature of the Madman himself, his hair wild, wearing big, round glasses, and with a car in the palm of each upheld hand.

There was a chance the guy I was meeting was already there, in the lot, watching me from between the cars. There was a chance he'd just drive up and make the exchange as fast as he could without even getting out of his car. There was a bigger chance that the phone would ring and he'd tell me where to go next. I figured the guy would probably drive by a few times just to be sure I was alone, and then he'd go to a phone he had picked out.

The phone rang. I picked it up.

"You have the package?" he asked. He had a high voice with maybe a hint of an accent.

"You know I do."

"Hold it up now so I can see it," he said.

I did nothing.

"Yes," he said. "I see it."

He was not very good at this game, but it was his game.

"You know where Elysian Park is?" he asked.

"I know."

"Go to the entrance on North Broadway," he said.

"The park closes at eight."

"About one hundred yards to your left, facing the front, is a service entrance," he said. "The gate will be unlocked. Drive in and close it behind you. You know how to get to the Memorial Grove?"

"Yeah."

"Go there now. Park. Walk toward the trees."

He hung up. I got back in the Crosley and started to drive. Elysian Park, on the north side of the city, covers about six hundred acres of land along the Los Angeles River. It has seven miles of paved roads with hairpin curves through arroyo-gashed hills, matted tangles of wild roses, creepers, blue gum eucalyptus, drooping pepper trees, and gnarled live oaks. There are ten miles of foot trails through canyons and up steep hills. The Memorial Grove is a neatly arranged grove of trees with bronze tablets laid out in memory of World War I dead.

I hadn't been to the park in five or six years, maybe more. My ex-wife and I had taken our lunch to the picnic grounds and walked down a path along the river. I thought about Anne for a few seconds. The city was full of memories of her. I turned on the radio. Music, sound. I didn't care. I hummed "Anything Goes." The band on the radio was playing "Stardust." The two didn't go together.

North Broadway wasn't busy, and I had no trouble finding the service entrance gate. I left the motor running, got out, opened the gate, went back to the car, and drove in. I got out again and closed the gates and got back in the Crosley. It was dark in front of me. My headlights were stronger than the bulbs in refrigerators, but not by much. I drove slowly, trying to remember the way to the Memorial Grove. I almost made a wrong turn, but my lights caught a sign with an arrow telling me which way to go.

I parked as close to the Memorial Grove as I could and got out. I had one hand on the .38 in my pocket and the other around the pouch of bills in the other pocket. A flashlight would have been a good idea. The moon wasn't giving me much help. I stood looking at the black outline of trees, leaves rustling from a thin breeze. I waited as my eyes adjusted to the darkness.

A spot of light. About thirty yards ahead and to my right. I watched it move toward me, disappearing a few times as it went by a tree between it and me. Then, about fifteen yards away, the light stopped moving.

"Come," came the voice behind the light, the same voice I had heard on the phone a half an hour earlier.

I moved toward the beam of light and felt it find my face.

"Show your hands," the voice said.

I did.

"Now show what you have brought me."

I took the pouch out of my pocket and held it up.

"Show me what you brought," I said, taking the .38 out of my other pocket.

There was a rustle behind the beam, and then a hand came out from behind it, holding an envelope.

"It's in here," he said. "Move forward slowly."

I did. When I was no more than a few yards from him, I could see his shape beyond the light. He was short, thin. He had hair. That was about all I could tell.

"We exchange at the same time," he said, holding his envelope out.

I followed his example.

His small hand went around the pouch, and my fingers touched his envelope. Things were going well so far, but that changed.

Two shots sounded from behind the beam of light. There was a man gasping. The flashlight fell and landed with its beam headed into the night. I got down on one knee and aimed into the darkness toward where I thought the gun shot had been fired from. I had no hope of hitting anyone. I was breathing hard, hard enough that I didn't hear whoever had come up behind me and hit me twice on the back of the head and neck.

It might have been more than twice. I was out after the second blow.

I've been knocked out before. The best part is being out. The worst part is coming to and feeling the pain. I felt a lot of pain. I was on my face, my neck hot, my head throbbing. I had grass in my mouth and something was crawling on my cheek. I brushed it away. It hurt to brush it away.

The flashlight was about six feet from me and still on, aimed at nothing. I crawled to it, took it in my left hand, and reached for my pocket, hoping the .38 was there. It wasn't. I stood, legs uninterested in cooperating, and pointed the beam toward the tree where I had made the exchange. It took me a few seconds to realize three things. First, I didn't have the envelope that had been handed to me. Second, I couldn't find the pouch with Cary Grant's money. Third, I saw my gun lying on the ground about a yard in front of a man sitting with his back against a tree.

He was almost paper white. Part of the reason was the cold beam of the flashlight, but part of it was because he was losing blood. Some of the blood was trickling out of his right ear. He was sitting in a small pool of his own blood.

I moved toward him, picked up my gun, and shone the flashlight in all directions. Nothing. No one. I knelt next to the little man, whose eyes rolled up toward my face. He said something, but it was so low I couldn't understand it, and, besides, it sounded like German.

"I don't understand German," I said.

His next words, the last he would ever speak, came out with a gurgle. He grasped my sleeve.

"George Hall," he said.

He let go of my sleeve and died. His eyes closed. His head slumped to the right.

The little man was wearing a watch. I turned his left wrist and pointed the beam at it. It was almost one. I sat down next to the dead man with my back against the same tree and put my gun on the ground between my legs.

Thoughts at the moment:

Get to a doctor. You were warned by Doc Hodgdon that you'd be in big trouble with another concussion.

My head, neck, and left shoulder hurt, really hurt, drumming, throbbing, beating damned hurt.

I should get the hell out of there.

Or, I should go find a phone and call the police.

Or, I should go find a phone and call Cary Grant and tell him what had happened.

What I decided to do was just sit there breathing hard on the cool grass. I looked over at the dead man and closed my eyes, not because I was looking at death but because of the pain. I forced myself to turn slightly and reach into his jacket pocket. He was wearing a light brown suit with a white shirt and a silk tie with alternating thin black, brown, and white stripes on a slight angle.

I found his wallet and looked through it.

Thirty-two dollars, three business cards, and a California driver's license. His name was Bruno Volkman. His address was in Burbank. I took out my notebook and scribbled the address. Then I pocketed the business cards, left the money in the wallet, and put it back in his pocket. I checked the other pockets. Nothing.

I still wasn't sure of what to do next other than try to get up and back to my car. Maybe I should crawl? No, I put my gun in my jacket pocket, held the flashlight in my left hand, and used the tree to help me stand. I was disoriented. It took me a few sweeps of the grove before I figured out where I had parked. I staggered in the right direction. I staggered right into a uniformed cop, who stepped back, one hand on the gun in his holster and the other on a flashlight he clicked on. He had steady eyes and a serious look on his face. I knew a lot of cops, but not many in this district and not this one.

"What're you doing in here?" he asked. "The park is closed."

I shook my head.

"That your car on the road? Crosley?"

"Yes."

"You hear any gunshots?" he asked.

"Gunshots," I repeated. "Well. . . ."

"How much have you had to drink?" he asked.

He thought I was drunk. I decided that it might be better that way. Then I decided that my decision was wrong. He was going to ask me for identification. He was going to find the dead man with what I was sure were a pair of holes in his back. If he didn't find the body tonight, someone would find him in the morning and then the police would find me.

"I had a Pepsi around ten-thirty," I said. "There's a dead man back there, sitting by a tree."

I nodded in the direction from which I had come.

The cop's gun was out now and aimed in my direction. He took a step back.

"You armed?" he asked.

I nodded to let him know I was.

"Right jacket pocket," I said. "I didn't shoot him. Someone shot him and hit me from behind. . . . Wait a second! Someone shot him from behind and someone hit me from behind. There had to be two of them."

Gun aimed at my stomach, the cop stepped forward and took the .38 from my pocket. He smelled the barrel.

"It hasn't been fired. Why are you carrying a weapon?"

"I'm a private investigator. I have a license."

"Show me."

I slowly fished my wallet out and handed it to him. He turned the flashlight on it, checked my identification and gun permit and then re-aimed the beam in my face.

"Let's go take a look at your dead man," the cop said.

"I need a doctor."

"We'll get you one," he said, herding me back toward the tree.

We had about forty yards to go. Every step was pure pain, from the electric padding that coated my feet to the jabs of agony at the top of my head. The cop, about six paces behind me, pointed the flashlight in front of him and scanned the trees.

"Which tree?" he asked.

I was pretty sure we were looking at it. There was no body.

"Someone took him," I explained.

"Took the dead guy, the one who was shot?"

"Looks that way," I said. "Check the tree and the ground."

"Stand right there," he said, moving to the tree and flicking his light on it and then on the nearby ground.

"Blood?" I asked.

"Blood," he confirmed.

He got up and moved in front of me.

"Turn around."

I turned.

"You've got a pretty big gash back there," he said. "Let's get you to a doctor."

"You think that's my blood on the tree?" I asked.

"What I think, between you and me and the wind, grass, and trees is that you came out here with a fruity friend and had a fight. He hit you and ran. We get a few like you every couple of months."

"I look like a? . . . " I was trying to understand.

"Call it whatever you like," he said. "You pansies come in all brands and sizes. Can you drive?"

"I think so," I said.

"Good. I'm going to do you a favor. Get in your car.

I'll drive behind you. You know where the hospital is?"

"County?"

"County. Drive there slow. I'll be right behind you. When I see you get out of your car at the hospital, I leave. What I want is for you to stay the hell out of this park and never come back. That or I take you in, and I don't have the time to fill out the papers. So, sure you can drive?"

"I can drive," I said.

"Let's go," he said. We trudged in the general direction of where I had parked.

CHAPTER 5

"I COULD, EXCEPT for the fact that you are walking unsteadily and talking incoherently, declare you legally dead."

The statement was made by an old acquaintance of mine, Dr. Marcus Parry, who seemed to live in the emergency room of Los Angeles County Hospital. He had seen me the last two times I had concussions. He agreed with my handball-playing friend, Doc Hodgdon, that I couldn't take any more blows to the head. Parry was just barely in his forties and back from the war for about a year. When he had left, he had been a lanky smiling man with blonde hair. When he came back, he had lost his smile and much of his hair. He looked ten years older than he was.

I was on an examining table, where he had stitched my scalp and checked my neck and shoulders. There was light coming through a white frosted pane of glass. There were three X rays hanging next to each other.

"They're in chronological order," he said. "This one." He pointed to the one farthest left. "This old four-year-old one shows depressions in the skull. Next one shows your skull beginning to look like an overused Ping-Pong ball. Let's jump to today's. Look."

I looked at it. It looked exactly like the others.

"I've seen healthier skulls on corpses exhumed after six months," Parry said. "And the scar tissue you've . . . what's the use? You're not going to change."

"It's what I do," I said.

"What you do. I see. Could you possibly consider doing something else?"

"What?"

"Cleaning toilets in the hospital would be a good start," he said flipping a switch and turning off the light behind the glass. "Safer and probably pays more than you make now."

"I'll think about it."

"No you won't," he said with a sigh, gathering his X rays of my head. "I've got a file on you, Peters. Someday I'll write an article about your body. You're a testament to what the human body outside of a war zone can take."

"Thanks."

"It wasn't a compliment. It was a comment on your stupidity."

"Determination," I amended.

He shook his head and motioned for me to follow him. I did. He had a tiny office with no windows. On his desk were three small bottles of pills.

"Take this one for pain," he said, handing me the first. "This one for balance. And this one for good luck. All three twice a day. Got it?"

"Got it," I said, picking up the bottles and putting them in my jacket pocket.

"How are you feeling?"

"Truth?"

"No," he said. "Lie to me. I'm the doctor. It's always best to lie to the doctor."

"I've felt better. Head still hurts. Shoulder's sore. But I can walk pretty steadily."

"Go home," he said, looking up at a nurse at his door. She might have been eighty or older. She motioned to him.

"Got to go," he said. "Busy tonight. Not like last night. New Year's Eve is always busy, but tonight's busy enough."

"Thanks, Doc," I said.

"Remain alive and I'll immortalize you in the annals of medicine," he said.

"I'll try."

He left shaking his head. I walked slowly to my car on legs that were willing to carry me but not too far. I got to Mrs. Plaut's on Heliotrope Street a little after three-fifteen in the morning. Parking was tough, but my car doesn't need much of an opening.

I climbed the porch steps and opened the door, turning my key as quietly as possible. Inside, I closed the door slowly and headed for the stairs.

Mrs. Plaut is nearly deaf but has a seventh or eighth sense. Even deep in sleep she knows when someone enters or leaves her boardinghouse. I had been lucky enough to escape her only five or six times when I'd come in very late at night or very early in the morning.

This time I wasn't lucky. She emerged from her apartment on my left, adjusting her white robe and her glasses at the same time.

"Mr. Peelers," she said. "Are you cognizant of the time?"

"Cognizant?"

"It's a 'Build Your Vocabulary' word from the *Reader's Digest*," she explained. "It means 'aware.'"

"I'm cognizant," I said. "I'm tired, sore, confused, and cognizant."

"You were fired?" she asked. "From which company?"

As I said, Mrs. Plaut thought I was a book editor who moonlighted as an exterminator. I had tried for over a year without success to straighten this out, or at least figure out how she had come to this conclusion, but I never got anywhere.

"I wasn't fired," I said.

"Good. You look terrible. Too much punch last night. Not enough sleep. It's on your table. In your room."

"The new chapter?" I guessed.

Mrs. Plaut was writing, in neat script on lined paper, the history of her family, and since I was an editor, it was my responsibility to read, approve, and respond to each chapter as she wrote it. Since criticism wasn't what she was after, I never pointed out that her book was disjointed and rambling. No actual editing was expected, either. But I had to read the chapters because every once in a while she'd ask me a question about what she had written.

"The new chapter," she said, folding her hands across her thin chest. "About the Sorenson twins and the incident at the gumbo restaurant in New Orleans."

"I can't wait to read it," I said, inching toward the stairs.

"The Sorensons were on my mother's side."

I was moving slowly upward, holding the railing so I wouldn't fall.

"They lived in Louisiana just after the War between the States," she said.

"Gumbo," I said.

"I'm not mumbling," she insisted.

I turned and repeated loudly, "Gumbo."

"Tomorrow is Sunday," she said.

I could have said that today was already Sunday, but I like to think I'm not a fool.

"Sunday brunch at ten," she said. "As always. Peanut butter-and-jelly omelettes and bread crumb-and-pecan biscuits. I'll awaken you at seven-thirty so you'll have plenty of time to wash up and shave and bathe."

I didn't want to get up at seven-thirty. I didn't want to get up all day. I wanted to lie on my mattress and feel sorry for myself. I had botched the job for Cary Grant. I was in pain. I didn't want a peanut butter-and-jelly omelette.

I smiled at Mrs. Plaut.

She smiled, went back into her rooms, and closed the door. I made it to my room on the second floor. The door wasn't locked. Locked doors weren't permitted in Mrs. Plaut's boardinghouse.

I didn't turn on the lights. I took off my clothes carefully and dropped them in the general direction of the closet. I groped my way to the mattress behind the sofa to my left, agonized it out, and flopped it on the floor. I found a pillow on the sofa and took it with me as I lay down in my undershorts. It took me about five minutes to find a position I could lie in so I wasn't in pain. Lying facedown would have worked. I had no bumps or bruises in front. The problem was I had a bad back I'd gotten a long time ago when I was protecting Mickey Rooney from a crowd at a premiere. A very large Negro gentleman had wanted to get close to Rooney. I'd tried to stop him. He'd picked me up in a bear hug and squeezed. My back has been a problem ever since. I had to sleep on it or risk waking up unable to do anything but crawl.

I was in a sort of curled-up baby position on my left side, facing the only window in my room. The window was open just enough so that Dash could get in if he felt like it.

I closed my eyes and opened them again quickly. The name. The dead guy. What was . . . Bruno Volkman. And the other name . . . George Hall. I knew I should get up, turn on the light, and write both names on something, but I told myself I'd remember. George Hall. Had Volkman told me the name of one of the people who had killed him, taken the envelope and Cary Grant's money?

The morning. I'd worry about it in the morning.

I dreamed of dead soldiers in World War I helmets coming out of a trench in Memorial Grove, bayonets at the ready, heading right for me across a no-man's land of trees, bomb shells, bodies, and rubble. I recognized the first one in the wave headed in my direction. It was the little guy who had been shot in the back. Then I recognized my brother, Phil, who'd been in that war. They looked grim. So did Koko the Clown, in full battle uniform.

Just before they got to me, I woke up with the explosion of a grenade a few yards away from where I stood in my underwear. Then they were gone and another grenade exploded nearby, but this time my eyes were open and I was staring at Mrs. Plaut, who was about to knock a third time.

"I'm awake," I said loudly, to stop her from sending another shock wave through my head.

The sun was shining through the window. I looked at the Beech-Nut Gum clock on my wall. Unlike my father's watch, it had always been within a minute or five of the right time. It said the time was seven.

"I have half an hour more," I shouted.

"You have a telephone call," she said. "Put on your britches and answer it."

"Who is it?" I asked, starting to test my head and neck with very slow movement.

"Archie something," she said. "Funny accent. Breakfast is at. . . ."

"Ten," I supplied, starting to sit up.

She nodded in approval and departed, leaving the door open. Getting up wasn't as bad as I thought it would be. It wasn't good either, but I knew who Archie was, Archie Leach, aka my client. Grant was proud of his actual name and tried to sneak it into his movies. Hitchcock did walk-ons in his own films, so why not Leach?

I got to my feet and felt each step as I moved toward the closet and my only robe, a gift from my sister-in-law, Ruth. It was thin, solid brown, and a little large, which was just the way I liked it.

The phone in Mrs. Plaut's boardinghouse is right near the stairway. The receiver was dangling, looking at me. I picked it up and said, "Peters."

"It's me," Grant said in his familiar voice.

"I know."

"What happened?" he asked.

I told him the story—the whole thing—and he said, "I'm sorry. I should have come with you. You said you got his name and that he mentioned another name before he died?"

I was afraid he would ask me that. I paused, hoping the names would come back to me.

"Give me a second," I said. "My brains are rattling around like a box of Wheaties."

Maybe a bowl of Wheaties would restore my memory. Maybe I'd have one before I went down to face Mrs. Plaut's breakfast.

"Peters, are you there?"

"I'm here. His name was George Volkman. No, not George. The other guy was George."

"Other guy?"

"The other guy whose name he gave me before he died. George Hall. The dead guy was Bruno Volkman."

I let out a puff of air in relief. I'd write the names in my notebook before I got dressed.

"Bruno Volkman," Grant repeated. "Bruno Volkman. Sounds familiar. You say he was short, thin?"

"Yes."

"I'll work on it. The name he gave you, George Hall."

"Right."

"I know Jon Hall and Huntz Hall," Grant tried. "There was a

woman named Estelle Hall who worked with me in a music hall act when I was a kid. We've got to find him."

We?

"Are you up to staying on the job?" he asked. "I'll pay your regular rates and expenses. This is important."

I wasn't sure if my body was ready, but my wallet was. So was my curiosity.

"I'm up to it."

"Good," he said. "You know where this Volkman lived?"

Then I remembered.

"I did get his name and address down in my notebook. I just remembered."

"You start there. I'll try to track down this George Hall. I'll call you later. Be careful. Did I tell you this is important?"

"You did."

"It is."

He hung up. So did I.

I went back to my room, picked up my pants, shirt, and jacket, and hung them in the closet. But first I took out my wallet, .38, car keys, and notebook and placed them on top of my dresser. My clothes needed cleaning.

I went to the lone bathroom the tenants shared, hoping they weren't up yet. I was in luck. I showered, shaved with my trustworthy old Gillette, brushed my teeth with the last of the powder in a little blue Dr. Lyons can, took the pills Doc Parry had given me, and opened the bathroom door.

Gunther, neat and waist-high to me, stood there patiently in his purple silk robe, his toiletries in a leather pouch in one hand and his white towel draped over his arm.

"Toby," he said, looking at me. "You have been hurt."

"I have been hurt," I confessed, "but it was only the first round. I'll tell you all about it after breakfast. The names Bruno Volkman or George Hall mean anything to you?"

He thought for a moment and said, "I do not think so. Would you like me to make inquiries?"

"If you don't mind."

"It is Sunday. I don't know what I can find, if anything, on Sunday, but I shall try."

I thanked him and made my way back to my room, where I checked my closet. I had choices. Not many, but choices. My new gray seersucker from Hy's was too good for what I had to do. I took the belt out of my crumpled pants and strung it through a pair of blue work pants. I picked a buttoned white shirt that had a stain in front. When I tucked it in, the stain wouldn't show. Once I was dressed, I opened my notebook to the page where I had written Volkman's address.

It looked like 778 Hauser. Hauser was just off of Pico. It could have been 990 Hauser though. I had written it in the dark, where sevens can become nines and an eight might be a zero with two strands of hair.

I went into the hall and picked up the phone book from the small rickety table. There was no phone listing for Bruno Volkman. I tried the operator. There still was no listing for a Bruno Volkman in Los Angeles.

I hung up and went down to breakfast. I was moving slowly. The pills from Parry seemed to be kicking into low gear. The descent wasn't painless, but it was possible. I had trouble moving my neck in spite of a hot shower, but I could live and work with that. No-Neck Arnie did.

The door to Mrs. Plaut's rooms was open. I knocked four times and went in. That was the custom at meals. I moved past Pistolero's cage. He screeched at me and bobbed his head up and down.

I ignored him and went into the dining room. I was the first to arrive. There was a pile of biscuits on a plate in the middle of the table and a coffee pot sitting on a thin block of polished wood. I sat at my usual place, poured some coffee, and tried to think.

Ben Bidwell and Emma Simcox came in together and nodded at me. He was wearing a sports jacket and tie. She was wearing a Sunday print dress.

"Some New Year's party," said the one-armed car salesman.

Most people don't work on Sunday, but Bidwell did. Sunday was a car-buying day, the busiest day of the week at Mad Jack's in Venice.

"Yeah," I said. "Why are so many car dealers insane?"

"Insane?" Bidwell said, sitting.

"Madman Sam, Crazy Bill, Mad Jack," I said as Emma Simcox sat.

"So you'll remember them," said Bidwell pouring a cup of coffee for Miss Simcox and himself. "And so you'll believe they're so crazy they'd give cars away."

"I can't tell one madman from another," I said.

"That's the truth," Bidwell said, reaching for a bread crumb-and-pecan biscuit. "Something wrong with your neck?"

"I got hit by a guy who had just shot another guy I was talking to in Elysian Park."

Bidwell smiled and shook his head. I always told him the truth. He thought I was an imaginative meal-table comedian.

Gunther arrived, fully dressed, in a three-piece suit, with a Windsor-knotted tie. He climbed up on his chair next to me.

"Good morning," he said, placing his napkin on his lap.

I had already seen Gunther this morning. Ben and Emma said, "Good morning."

"Toby, I paused on the way to look at the telephone book," Gunther said. "I found two George Halls in the Los Angeles directory and one in Burbank. I shall endeavor to find out more about them."

"I knew a George Hall," Bidwell said, eating a muffin, cup of coffee in hand. "Mechanic."

"Where does he live?" asked Gunther.

"Doesn't. He's dead. War. This war, not mine."

Mrs. Plaut came in from the kitchen with the first two neatly folded omelettes. I could smell peanut butter. She pushed the first one onto Emma Simcox's plate with a spatula and then served the second one to Bidwell.

"Be right back," she said, hurrying out again.

Bidwell took a small tentative piece of the omelette on his fork and ushered it into his mouth. We all waited, trying to gauge the look on his face.

"Good," he said. "A little weird, but good."

Emma Simcox began to eat. She nodded in agreement.

Mrs. Plaut came back with omelettes for Gunther and me. And then she was off to the kitchen again.

The omelette wasn't bad. Mrs. Plaut returned and took her seat. There was no omelette on her plate.

"Where's yours?" Bidwell asked.

"Peanut butter and jelly in an omelette?" Mrs. Plaut answered, as she often did, with a question. "Doesn't sound appetizing."

All of us knew better than to pursue this. We ate our breakfast silently. I was starting to get up when Mrs. Plaut said, "A prayer."

I sat back down. We'd never had a prayer before.

"Amen," said Bidwell.

"Wait till I say the prayer and then you say 'Amen,'" Mrs. Plaut said.

"Sorry," said Bidwell, amused.

Mrs. Plaut put her palms together and looked up. She reminded me of a Norman Rockwell painting. The whole scene reminded me of a Norman Rockwell painting. Her eyes moved to each of us. We put our palms together, fingers pointing up.

"Dear Lord," she began. "I had a friend who was Japanese. Yoko Mirimi. Now she's in a camp somewhere. I won't ask you why. You made a mistake when you gave us free will. We don't use it well. Just look at the Japs and the Nazis. It is a New Year and we have gathered at your table to each make a resolution."

Mrs. Plaut looked up. Her eyes fell on Ben Bidwell. He was amused.

"I resolve in the coming year to turn up the charm and sell a record number of cars."

"I resolve," Emma Simcox said softly, "to not judge people till I know them."

"I resolve," said Gunther, "to learn Bulgarian."

It was my turn.

"I resolve," I said, "to do my damnedest not to get hit on the head or neck or any other part of my anatomy."

"Amen," said Mrs. Plaut. And we all said, "Amen."

"My chapter on the Sorenson twins," she said, rising and looking at me.

"I'll read it today."

"I am growing no younger," she said, reaching for Gunther's empty plate.

"I'm cognizant of that," I said.

Before she turned and headed for the kitchen, I think she allowed herself a small smile.

CHAPTER

BRUNO VOLKMAN'S APARTMENT was at 778 Hauser. The name "Volkman" was on his mailbox. The building was a two-story white adobe. His apartment was on the second floor. There was another apartment next to his.

I didn't bother to knock. I remembered Ted Lewis in some movie tipping his top hat to the side and singing, "We never knock 'cause nobody's there."

I hummed "Me and My Shadow" as I examined the lock. Simple spring model. I was reaching into my pocket for my knife when I turned the doorknob. It was open. I went in.

The Sunday sun was bright, but all the lights were on in the combination living and dining room where I stood. I closed the door behind me, my hand on my .38.

Bruno Volkman kept a neat apartment. The kind of furniture that looked like the set of an Astaire–Rogers movie. Lots of white and black and chrome steel. Two paintings on the wall, one all squares and cubes in black on white and the other a super-streamlined train, racing from left to right, leaving a trail of smoke behind it.

I moved to the kitchen, also neat, and opened the door to what I assumed was the bedroom. It was. The blinds were closed. I turned on the light. Double bed made with a light blue cover with matching blue pillows. A dresser. A night table next to the bed, with a telephone and a radio. There was a single picture on the wall, a big one, a painting of Katharine Hepburn cradling white flowers in her arms. On the dresser were two framed photographs. One was of a skinny little boy in short pants being hugged by a woman wearing a distinctly turn-of-the-century dress and hat. The other photograph was a recent one of Bruno Volkman and another man, somber, shoulder-to-shoulder, looking straight at the camera.

There was one more door. I opened it. It was a closet with clothes neatly hung and evenly spaced, shoes lined up on the low shelf over the clothes. That was it except for the body of Bruno Volkman sitting behind the clothes when I parted them. His mouth was open and he was looking at my knees.

I closed the closet door and started to look through the dresser, which was just as neat as the rest of Volkman's apartment. Even his underpants were folded flat.

In the bottom drawer I found a box, took it out, and put it on the bed. The box was filled with pro–Nazi and Bund literature. Almost all of it was in English. I checked for photographs, maybe notes. Nothing but the literature. I was scanning a pamphlet to see if he had marked anything when I heard the front door of the apartment open.

I stuffed the pamphlet back in the box, put the box back in the drawer, closed the drawer, and walked through the door, past the small kitchen, and into the living room, where I stood facing two men, both in their late forties or early fifties, both wearing hats, both on the hefty side.

"I didn't hear you knock," I said, my hand in my pocket grasping my gun.

"We didn't knock," one man said. "Door was open. Who are you?"

"Conrad Bishop," I said.

"We're Kelso and O'Boylan, Los Angeles police. Name by the bell says Volkman. Where is he and what are you doing here?"

"Visiting," I said. "Bruno left the door open for me. He should be back any minute."

"Identification," said the cop who I guessed was Kelso.

I fished out my wallet and handed it to him. He flipped it open.

"Tobias Leo Pevsner," he read from my driver's license. "And you've got a private investigator's card. It doesn't say Conrad Bishop. Pevsner? You related to Captain Phil Pevsner at the Wilshire District?"

"My brother," I said. I didn't bother to tell him that Phil had been reduced to lieutenant less than a year ago.

The two cops looked at me.

"Conrad Bishop is my stage name," I explained. "I use it all the time. It's what people in the business call me."

"You're an actor," said O'Boylan.

"Acting, singing, a little dancing," I said. "All background stuff. You see *Follow the Fleet*? The one where Fred Astaire's a sailor?"

"Yeah," said Kelso.

"Remember when Ginger Rogers falls into a sailor's arms at the end of one of the numbers?" I asked.

"'I'm Putting All My Eggs in One Basket,'" said O'Boylan.

"I was the sailor."

"I think I would have remembered seeing a face like yours if it was you," said Kelso.

"Makeup," I said.

"You're not a private investigator?"

"I am, but I haven't really worked at it since I decided to go into the movies."

This was not going well. I should have told the truth, but lying comes so easily when you find a body with bullet holes.

"Have a seat," said Kelso.

I sat.

"I'll look around," Kelso left me seated with O'Boylan, who folded his hands in front of him and watched me.

Kelso was back before I could figure out what I would say.

"We got a call saying a man had been murdered here," said Kelso. "There's a dead man in the closet, Pevsner."

"It's Peters, Toby Peters. That's my legal name now," I said. "I came here to see Volkman, found him dead, and panicked. I'm carrying a gun, but it hasn't been fired."

O'Boylan moved directly in front of me and motioned for me to stand up. I did. He had no trouble finding my weapon.

"You know what I think?" asked Kelso.

I didn't know, so I kept my mouth shut.

"I think we're going to call the M.E. and take you over to the Wilshire for a family get-together," Kelso said.

On the way to the Wilshire station, nobody said a word.

"Let me be sure I've got this straight," my brother Phil said when I was seated across from him in his small office. "You were driving in Elysian Park last night. You went to the Memorial Grove."

"I felt an urge to honor the war dead," I said. "It just came over me."

"Very patriotic," he said, and then looked down at the notes he had taken. "You ran into another guy in the Grove. He told you his name was Bruno Volkman. Suddenly someone you didn't see shot him in the back and hit you on the head."

"Yes."

"And," Phil went on, rubbing one hand over his short, bristly gray hair, "when you woke up, Volkman's body was gone."

"Yes, you can ask the cop who found me there," I said.

"I've got Montoya looking for your cop," he said, sitting back.

Phil was a broad-shouldered, heavy-set man in his fifties. He had a wife, Ruth, who was dying, and two sons. He also had a temper, which had gotten him into trouble more than once and cost him his captain's badge. When we were kids, I had been Phil's punching bag of choice. Things had stayed that way until a little over a year ago. While Ruth wasted away, Phil grew mellow and I stopped trying to provoke him. So I was fairly sure he wasn't going to throw anything at me or come over the desk to slam me against the wall. He had done both on more than one occasion.

He just sat there.

"You were there in the park on a case," he said finally, rubbing the bridge of his nose with a thumb and finger.

"I . . ."

"Don't give me your crap about going to Memorial Grove in a sudden burst of nostalgia."

". . . and patriotism," I added.

"Toby," he said evenly, "Don't make me return to the bad old days. Don't make me do something I won't regret for a second. Who is your client and what were you doing in the park?"

"I didn't kill him," I said.

"Preliminary report says he's been dead at least ten hours, and Kelso and O'Boylan found blood traces on the floor. I can't see you killing him last night and bringing his body home and then sticking around for ten hours till the police came."

"And what about the tip that said there was a dead man in the apartment?" I asked. "My guess is someone was watching the place or following me and called in so I'd be there when Kelso and O'Boylan arrived."

"Sounds right," said Phil, leaning forward with his elbows on the desk.

He sat there staring at me.

"What?" I asked.

"Your client's name and the real reason you were in the park."

"Can't tell you, Phil," I said.

"Did Volkman get killed because you met him in the Grove?"

"Can't tell you, Phil," I said again.

"It's a crime to obstruct justice," he said.

"I know."

"And I know you know," he said. "You're not giving me much choice here, Toby."

"My client didn't kill Volkman," I said.

"You're sure?"

"I'm sure," I said.

"Good," said Phil, slapping his hands on the desk, a sure sign that he was about to lose control. "Now *I* want to be sure."

"My word's not good enough, is it?"

He didn't bother to answer. He was on his feet now, fists clenched.

"I'd tell you if I could," I said. "But I promised I'd keep my client out of this. If I start turning my clients in, it won't be long before there aren't any clients. Phil, I sell my loyalty."

"You want me to make you an offer?" he said with heavy sarcasm.

"I don't betray my clients," I said.

"Integrity."

"That's all I have, that and a body in serious need of an overhaul and some rest."

Phil came around the desk. I got up quickly, ready to get the hell out of that office before he threw me into a corner. He cut me off and moved in front of me. His right hand came up and touched my arm.

"How badly did they pound you?" he asked.

"Bad enough. Stitches. Sore neck and shoulder."

"I'll have to turn you over to the district attorney's office," he said.

"They haven't got enough to hold me," I said. "And if you just talk to the cop at the park, he'll tell you I reported the murder."

Phil backed away, shaking his head. He moved to his desk and picked up the phone.

"Lester," he said, "find me the officer on duty last night who checked out Elysian Park. . . . I don't have his name. He's an old-timer. Make it fast."

"You want coffee?" he asked, hanging up the phone.

"No, thanks."

Phil shrugged and left to get himself a cup. I wasn't thinking straight. I had handled the two cops badly and I wasn't doing all that well with Phil. I reached into my pocket for my three bottles of pills and downed one from each as Phil returned to his desk.

His phone was ringing. He put the cup down and picked up the phone.

"Yeah," he said. "Yeah . . . you sure? . . . Thanks."

He hung up the phone, took a sip of coffee, and looked at me.

"No cop in the park last night," he said.

"He was there," I said.

"Park's not patrolled at night," said Phil.

"He said . . . " I began. Then I stopped. "He let me go. Said he didn't want to do the paperwork."

Phil stared at me.

"You know I'm beginning to think the guy wasn't a cop. I'm beginning to think he was just trying to find out what I knew."

"Think some more, Tobias," Phil said.

"I know."

"But I believe you," he said after a long pause. "I know when you're lying. And I know you wouldn't shoot anyone in the back. But you do know something."

I shrugged.

"All right," he said with a final sigh, "we'll let the D.A.'s office take over."

"I want to call my lawyer," I said.

"Give me his number," said Phil. "I'll get him for you."

"It's Sunday," I said. "We'll have to call him at home. I don't know his home number, and only his business phone is listed in the phone book."

Phil nodded. He knew who my lawyer was. He called the phone company, talked to a supervisor, and came up with a home number for Martin Raymond Leib.

Marty Leib's wife answered the phone. I told her I had to talk to her husband. She sighed and put the phone down. I could hear her call out, "Martin, you have a call. I think it's one of your criminals."

Then Marty came on.

"Who is it?" he asked.

"Toby Peters," I said. I told him where I was and gave him the broad outline.

"Wilshire Station?" he repeated.

"Yes."

"I have to shower," he said. "I was playing tennis."

"Sorry," I said.

"Don't be. Your bill will reflect the inconvenience."

"Happy New Year," I said.

"The same to you," he answered and hung up.

Three hours later I was on the street in front of the station. Marty Leib, all three hundred pounds of him in a lightweight white suit, said, "Much of my income is derived from police and attorneys working for the city, county, or state who don't know the basic criminal law."

I nodded. I was free. Marty had shown up with a writ. How he got it so quickly was a question I didn't want to ask. The assistant

D.A. Phil had turned me over to was a kid four years out of law school. Ten minutes after my rotund lawyer entered the office Marty had the poor guy apologizing for detaining me.

"You'll have my bill within two days," he said. "As you know, I prefer cash. Is there anything else I can do for you?"

"Give me a ride to my car," I said.

"Where is it?"

I told him where Volkman's apartment was, and he said it wasn't out of his way. I asked if he planned to charge me for the ride. He said he would throw it in free.

"Play tennis, Peters?" he asked.

"No."

I tried to imagine Marty in shorts waddling around a tennis court.

"Great game," he said. "A game of the mind."

"Is everything a game of the mind?"

"It is if you know how to manipulate the rules," he said with a laugh that I felt down to the last dollar in my wallet.

CHAPTER 7

MARTY LEFT ME in front of Volkman's apartment building.

"I advise against it," he'd said as I opened the car door.

"What?"

"Going back into Volkman's apartment."

"I wasn't going to."

"You were considering it."

"Maybe."

"Don't. There are limits even to my ability to play along the edges of the law." I'd watched him drive away. Then I looked up at Volkman's apartment. The temptation was there. I resisted it and reached into my pocket for my wallet.

I had taken three business cards from Volkman's body the night before. I had glanced at them this morning hoping one of them would say something like, "Wolf Larsen, Kit-Kat Club" or "Adolph Obermenchen, Exporter-Importer." Clues like that led radio and movie detectives to interesting or colorful places where they could make wise-guy conversation, push a few people around, and get past a tough beautiful girl to a tough-talking scene and a shoot-out with the murderer.

One of Volkman's cards read: "Jacklyn Wright, School of Performance, Caroll College, Burbank, California" There was a phone number. The second card read: "Wesley Flynn, Typewriter Repair and Maintenance." His address was almost downtown and his phone number in big letters. The third and final card read: "Jack Baron, Baron Radios and Phonographs. All major manufacturers. Best prices." Jack Baron's address was on La Cienega.

I drove to the Regal drugstore where Anita was working. She was talking to two ancient women who were taking their time with Cokes and toasted cheese sandwiches. Anita spotted me, excused herself, and moved toward me.

"The Tomlin sisters," she said. "They think they're related to Pinky Tomlin, but they're not sure."

The smile on Anita's face disappeared when she took a longer look at me.

"What happened?"

"Got mugged in the park last night," I said. "There were at least eight of them. I sent most of them to the hospital, and the others ran in fear. They'll know better than to tangle with Toby Peters again."

"Toby," she said with resignation.

I shrugged.

"Guy I was meeting in the park on business got shot. I got clobbered from behind. Sore neck and shoulders, a few stitches. I didn't get my business done, and I was found in the dead guy's apartment this morning. The police had questions. I had a headache."

"Is this all true?" she asked.

"True," I said. "Dead guy was named Bruno Volkman. Gave me a name before he died, George Hall. I've got clues all over the place, names, cards, the memory of the face of a fake cop who either shot Volkman or hit me."

"So what more do you need?" she asked.

"Coffee," I said.

She nodded and moved to get me a mug. She was generous with both the cream and sugar. I don't love coffee, but the cream and sugar made up for it, and the caffeine jolt was what I needed.

"It hurt?" she asked, touching my hand.

"Would I come here for pity if it didn't hurt?"

"You can't turn your head can you?"

"Sure, if I love agony," I said, taking a gulp of hot coffee.

"Toby, sometimes I think you do love a little agony."

A new customer, a fat guy I had seen in the drugstore before, came in and sat three stools down. He nodded at me. I nodded back. Anita moved over to take his order. I thought about what Anita had said. A little agony wasn't a bad thing. Some people only have to be pinched a little to know the world is real. I seem to require a good crack on the head or nose.

I finished my coffee. Anita came back to fill my cup.

"Mr. Karsinian is having his usual," she whispered. "Chicken salad on white, extra mayo, a side of cole slaw, and a vanilla shake. Three days a week for the last year or more."

"Some people need a routine," I said.

"Some people," she said, pointing a finger at me, "need their head examined."

"Mine was. Eight stitches. Movie Thursday night still on?" I asked.

"Think you can raise your head enough to see the screen?"

"We'll get there early and sit in the back. Pick you up at seven?"

"Seven," she said, glancing over her shoulder as two slices of toast popped up in the toaster. I took my bill, picked up a 100-tablet bottle of Bayer aspirin for fifty-nine cents as back-up for the pain pills Doc Parry had given me, and paid on the way out.

I called Violet who spent one Sunday a month doing the billing, and asked her if there had been any calls.

"A Mr. Leach," she said. "Wants you to call him. Says you have his number. And Gunther. Didn't leave a message."

"Thanks, Violet," I said.

"Tuesday night, Eddie Booker's fighting Paul Hartnek in Oakland," she said.

"I'm not betting with you anymore, Violet," I said. "You've destroyed my confidence."

Violet's husband, Rocky, was a promising middleweight whose career was on hold while he served in the Pacific. I knew boxing. Violet knew it better. She had won every bet we had made on a fight for the past year.

"Hartnek weighed in at one hundred and seventy-nine to Booker's one-seventy," she said.

"Which one do you want?" I asked.

"Booker," she said. "I'll give you two to one he takes it and the fight doesn't go the distance."

"No."

"Three to one," she said. "Hartnek has a record of. . . ."

"I know," I said. "No bet."

"Four to one," she said.

"Fight doesn't go the distance? Booker wins?"

"Right."

"Five dollars."

"Five dollars."

If I won, I'd only be behind by about eighty dollars in bets with Violet Gonsenelli.

"Shelly there?"

"Dr. Minck is with a patient."

"I don't hear screaming."

"Mr. Polar is mercifully unconscious," she said. "And Dr. Minck is singing 'Somewhere I'll Find You.'"

I left it at that and called Mrs. Plaut's. Gunther answered the hall phone after eight rings.

"Anything on George Hall?" I asked.

"So far, a butcher on Boyle Avenue and a man on Franklin Avenue. I don't know his profession or work," he said. He gave me their addresses. "I shall broaden my search."

"Thanks, Gunther," I said. "I'll get back to you."

Cary Grant didn't answer the phone. A woman did, and I asked if Grant was there.

"Who's calling?"

"Toby Peters."

"And you're calling about? . . . "

"A U.S.O. appearance."

She said she would get him and put down the phone. I watched people walking by, cars driving by, and time passing by. Eventually Grant picked up the phone.

"Mr. Peters. So glad you called. My wife says you want to talk about the U.S.O. show."

"You can't talk, can you?"

"I'm afraid not," he said cheerfully.

"Volkman's body was found in his apartment," I said. "So was I."

"Sorry to hear that."

"I've got a good lawyer and I'm back on the street. I've got some possible leads to George Hall. Don't know how good they are, but. . . ."

"Yes, check on those by all means," he said.

"Volkman," I said. "Did you figure out where you might have seen him?"

"I'm afraid not," Grant said.

"Can I call you later?"

"Of course I'll call you later," Grant said. "Though we really do have to talk in person. Shall we say your office, four?"

"Four," I repeated.

"See you then," he said and hung up the phone.

I made a list: the two George Halls and the three places on the cards from Volkman's wallet.

The butcher was nearest. I listened to *The Romance of Helen Trent* on the radio and tried to think about what I was going to say. I briefly considered and rejected, "Pardon me but are you a Nazi spy?" or "All right Hall, or whatever your real name is, we know who you are. Make it easier on yourself and give up."

I had little confidence in that approach. I decided to play it as it came to me, which would depend on how Hall the butcher looked, sounded, and talked.

Helen Trent sounded worried about someone named Tom. Helen Trent sounded tired. I knew how she felt.

I switched to the news. A U.S. destroyer had sunk in lower New York harbor early in the morning. There were one hundred and sixty-three known survivors, including one hundred and eight injured. The origin of the accident was not yet known. The Royal Air Force had hit Berlin for the tenth successive night of bombing. And six-foot-eight George Mikan of the DePaul Blue Demons was leading the nation, averaging seventy points a game.

There was a small parking lot next to Hall and Croft's Quality Meats on Boyle Avenue. The lot had spaces for eight cars, with a sign posted, saying "These spaces are reserved for customers of Hall & Croft's and Meridian Gift Shop."

I parked next to a Ford coupe with a dented right fender and moved to the street entrance of Hall & Croft's. When I opened the door, the place smelled of sawdust and blood. There are two kinds of blood smells. The kind that sighs death and violence, and the neutral, almost sweet, smell of fresh meat. This was the fresh meat smell. Two women were ahead of me at the glass display case, where a surprising number of cuts of red meat were lined up neatly.

The butcher behind the counter wore a white apron only slightly soiled with blood. He kept wiping his hands on the apron, his eyes fixed attentively on the woman across the counter who was saying, "Do I have enough coupons left for two small lamb chops?"

She was thin, tight-lipped, and clutching a small black purse in both hands.

"No," said the butcher, a big man with wispy blonde hair, a pink face, and thick hands.

"Then what?"

"Half-pound of ground beef."

"It's not too fat?"

"It's ground beef," the butcher said.

The woman next to me, young, dark hair pulled back, and wearing a red-and-white bandana, whispered. "We're at his mercy."

"Yes," I said.

"Butcher's are like gods. It's the war."

"I know," I said nodding at the butcher. "Is that George Hall?"

"It's George Hall," the young woman said softly, with a sigh. "The war will be over soon and the reign of the butcher god will be over."

"You're a student?" I asked.

"Riveter," she said. "I read a lot. You?"

"Private detective."

"Let me guess," she said. "George has been chopping up customers and selling them as ground beef."

"I don't think so," I said as the woman at the counter accepted her package of meat wrapped in brown paper and tied with a string.

"Next," said George Hall.

Did I hear an accent? Did I imagine one?

The young woman moved forward and gave George Hall her

order, handing him the appropriate stamps. He pulled a piece of meat from the display case, put it on the block of wood behind the counter, and cleaved it cleanly in half with a single blow.

"What else?"

"Nothing," the young dark-haired woman said, looking at me. She gave a slight shake of her head to indicate that she had no say in the matter of butcher Hall's shopkeeping graces.

She paid and moved past me.

"Next," Hall said. I moved forward to face him over the counter.

I had no plan, no tricks, just a plunge ahead to see what his reactions might give away.

"A friend of mine said I should see you," I said. "Said you'd have a good deal for me."

Hall glared at me, unblinking.

"His name is Bruno Volkman."

Hall looked at me blankly.

"He said you were the man I was looking for, that a lot of people were looking for."

"People?" asked Hall.

"The FBI has a lot of people."

"If somebody is looking for me, I am always here," he said. "Who are you?"

"A friend of Bruno Volkman."

"I know no Bruno Volkman," Hall said, wiping his hands on his apron. "I sell meat. I'm a butcher."

"Bruno Volkman is dead," I tried.

"Many people are dead," Hall said. "Many people. I think you are a crazy person. I think you should leave now."

"We're not finished," I said.

Hall picked up his cleaver. There were traces of blood on the shining steel.

"We are finished," he said.

"Who's on the list and where's the money?"

"I'm calling the police on you," he said, moving toward a phone on the wall. "You are a crazy person."

"I'm not going to give up until you tell me what I want to know," I said, beginning to think this was not the George Hall I was looking for. This George Hall picked up the phone while he looked at me, cleaver still in his hand.

"I know how to buy and cut meat," he said. "I know how to sell meat. I know that there are people who call names behind my back at me and my wife and my children because I am born a German. You people care nothing that I am now American, that my son Gerhardt is a sergeant in American army. That is what I know, crazy man."

He started to dial a number and I said, "I think I made a mistake."

"You think? Go away. Do not return."

I decided to follow his advice and hurried out the door into the morning light.

The next stop was the George Hall who lived on Franklin. I didn't know what he did or if he was at work, but I found his address in an eight-flat apartment building and knocked at the door.

"Who is it?" an odd squeaky voice asked.

"Name is Rasmussen. Seymour Rasmussen. I have to see Mr. George Hall about a billing error."

"Georgie owes you money?" the squeaky voice asked. "No surprise. He owes everybody. Can't hold on to a dollar bill. Money comes alive in his pocket and crawls away."

"Is Mr. Hall home?" I asked.

"Of course," the squeaky voice answered.

"Well, can I see him?"

"If you have a strong heart and stomach," the voice answered. "He'll open the door."

And the door did open.

In front of me stood a thin man in a droopy gray robe. His dark hair was disheveled and his eyes were wide and bewildered. He pulled the door all the way open and fiddled with the sash of his robe. He had a small dark bottle in his hand. I looked down at his feet. They were bare. He held up the small bottle.

"Vicks Va-tro-nol," he said. "I think I'm coming down with a cold."

"George Hall?" I asked.

"Yes," he said. "Are you going to beat me up?"

"Why would I beat you up?"

He shrugged and gulped and stepped back. I followed him into a large room filled with bookcases, old overstuffed furniture with faded purple and blue patterns, and cardboard boxes piled neatly, about chest high in the middle of the room.

"Going somewhere?" I asked.

He looked puzzled.

"The boxes?"

"Oh, yes. I mean no. I just haven't unpacked yet."

"You just moved in?"

"I think it will be a year next month," he said, looking at the boxes and adjusting his sash again. "But I might have to move. Hard to get steady work in our line."

"Your line?"

"Bobby and me," he said.

And then his voice changed, his lips came together and he said in the voice I had heard through the door, "The world doesn't appreciate a talent like ours."

If George Hall was a ventriloquist, he was a terrible one. The voice was fine, but he moved his lips. Then again, so did Edgar Bergen.

"You're a ventriloquist," I said.

"I do voices," said Hall in his own voice. "I play parties for kids, do bars and nightclubs as a ventriloquist, but that's not my talent. I'm more like Mel Blanc. I do voices."

And he proceeded to do voices.

"Hey gringo, what you want from me, eh?" was delivered deep and raspy.

"You wouldn't want to scare a little girl now, would ya, huh?" came a little girl's voice.

"Zo, vas is it zat you vant from me?" he demanded in a deep Germanic growl.

"No want trouble from white man," he said in a slow tenor that reminded me of Tonto on the radio.

"Enough," I said. "You're very talented."

"Radio," he said. "That's what I'm born for. You want something to drink? I've got Green River in the refrigerator."

"No thanks."

"I'll have one," he said. "Have a seat."

I sat on the sofa. It smelled stale and was lumpy with wild springs. Hall came back almost immediately. He had poured the soda into a tall glass. We both watched it fizzle for a few seconds, and then he sat across from me and leaned forward, glass held tightly in two hands.

"I can pay," he said.

"Pay?"

"Pay whatever it is I owe you," he said. "You said you were here about a bill. I just got a lot of money."

"A lot of money?"

"Two hundred dollars," he said. "One night's work."

"Doing what?"

"Murder," he said. He took a swallow from his glass.

"Bruno Volkman," I said.

He looked at me for an instant, and in a variation on his German accent of a few minutes earlier, he said, "I know nothing of what it is you seek. Nothing. There is no point in torturing me. My life belongs to mine Fuhrer."

"That was? . . . "

"Bruno Volkman," he said.

"You know Bruno Volkman?"

"No, you gave me a name. It sounded German. I . . ."

"Murder. You said you murdered someone."

His eyes opened wide.

"No, I said I got two hundred dollars for *Murder*, a one-hour radio show. *Lux Presents Hollywood*. The entire cast got locked in the wrong studio. I was there to do one voice, a barmaid. Then they handed me the script and told me to do the whole thing, all the parts but Herbert Marshall's. He was there. Kept looking at me and smiling. You know he only has one leg?"

"I know."

"Nice guy. Marshall. You listen to *A Man Called X* on the radio? That's Marshall, and Leon Belasco plays Pagon Zelshmidt. I can do that accent."

"You said 'murder.' Whose?"

"Not who, what. *Murder*, an Alfred Hitchcock movie. Maybe they'll give me more work now."

"I think I have the wrong George Hall," I said.

Hall nodded and looked at his bottle of Va-tro-nol for a second and then said,

"Colds, sore throats," he said. "Piano players worry about their hands. My voice is my income."

"Take care of yourself," I said and went out the door.

"I've got 666 Cold Tablets too," he added.

As soon as the door closed, I heard the Bobby voice, high and squeaky, say, "You never found out what he wanted. He's gonna come back and rob us. Why don't you listen to me once in a while?"

I had exhausted my George Halls. Maybe Gunther had turned up more. It was getting close to four in the afternoon. I got in my car and headed for the Farraday Building.

On the radio, I learned that anti-Jewish vandals were at work in New York City and had attacked more than one synagogue. I also learned that Japanese prisoners were saying that the Japanese were sick of war and were no longer confident of victory. And I heard about the newly formed Women's Auxiliary of the Brush-Off Club. The Brush-Off Club had been started by soldiers who had been jilted by their girlfriends back home. Now a group of women in Santa Monica had started their auxiliary of women who had been jilted by servicemen. I wondered what they did at their meetings.

There were no parking spaces within a block of the Farraday. It was a busy Monday, the day after a holiday weekend. I was heading back to park at No-Neck Arnie's when a Cadillac pulled out in front of Manny's Tacos. I parked and went into Manny's.

Manny stood behind the counter, reading the paper, his round belly threatening to pop through his shirtfront. He was smoking a Camel and squinting at the sports section.

There were a few customers, and the radio was playing a Christmas song.

"Christmas is over," I said.

Manny grunted but didn't look up from his paper.

"Christmas was over when they hit Pearl Harbor," he said. "It'll stay over until the Nazis and Japs give up. What can I do you for?"

"Six tacos, the works," I said.

He put down the paper and moved toward the grill at the rear of the shop.

"Juanita was looking for you," he said. "Says she has something to tell you. You weren't in your office. She thought you might be here."

I sat on one of the round swivel stools at the counter while I waited.

I didn't plan to go running to Juanita the Seer for confusing predictions I could do nothing about. Once she had told me to beware of mashed potatoes. So I stopped eating mashed potatoes. Two weeks later, a waiter at Delio's on Fairmont tripped and dropped a bowl of mashed potatoes on my lap. I never saw him coming. There was nothing I could have done about it. Someone else had ordered them. I wasn't going to give up mashed potatoes again.

"We've got a secret weapon," Manny said. "You hear about it?"

"Heard something," I said.

"Yeah," said Manny. "I hear it's a cannon that can shoot big bombs a hundred miles from a destroyer off of Japan and hit any city we want. That's what I heard."

He placed the tacos in a brown paper bag. They smelled of heat and chili peppers. I paid him.

"Big bombs," I said.

"Can shoot 'em from a hundred miles away."

"We should check it out with Juanita," I said, turning toward the door.

"I did," said Manny. "She said it isn't a big bomb. It's a little boy. Our secret weapon is a little boy."

Manny shook his head, and I left and walked from the corner to the Farraday. A man wearing sunglasses and a woman wearing a black hat with a wide brim that hid her face in shadows were coming out, talking about a song.

"Who can sing that?" she said.

"Ginny, you can sing that," the man said.

I think it was Ginny Simms, maybe.

The vast cavern of the Farraday hummed and rattled with voices, music, clacking typewriters, and sounds I didn't recognize. Late on a Monday afternoon. Everything was normal except for the office of Sheldon Minck.

Violet wasn't at her desk in the little waiting-reception room. No one was in the room, but inside, on Shelly's chair sat an enormous man with a dark beard. Dr. Sheldon Minck had one knee on the man's chest and a tight grip on the pliers or whatever it was he held in his hand.

"Biggest I've ever seen, Toby," he said, glancing at me, his glasses perched at the end of his nose and slipping fast. "I'm going to mount it."

"Like a fish," I said.

"Sure."

The giant in the chair sat with his hands at his sides. He seemed to be snoring gently.

"He's out," Shelly said. "Friend of Jeremy's. Wrestler. The Mountain. Famous."

"Never heard of him," I said, skeptical about Jeremy sending any friend of his to the sixth-floor-forceps-wielding escapee from dental hell.

"I feel like . . . like Captain Abe on top of Moby Dick," Shelly said, wiping his brow with his soiled sleeve.

"Ahab," I corrected. "And Ahab never caught Moby Dick. Moby Dick killed him."

"He did?" asked Shelly, pausing for an instant. "Just goes to show you."

"Show me what?"

"Don't look for happy endings," he said with a great grunt and a two-handed pull.

Something went "pop" and Shelly flew back, two hands still clinging to the pliers.

"Got it," he said.

It was a damn big tooth.

"I'm going to clean it and mount it," he said, adjusting his glasses as he got up. "Or maybe I should hang it inside of a glass box."

"First you might want to stop your patient from bleeding to death."

"Right, right," he said, moving to the sleeping, snoring Mountain, putting the tooth carefully on the nearby tray and picking up a white gauze pad that looked more or less clean.

I moved to my cubbyhole office door.

"You've got people waiting," he said, stuffing the scrunched piece of gauze into the hole from which the massive tooth had been plucked. "Gunther and that other guy from yesterday, the one who looks like George Kaplan. Man's got good teeth, but even almost perfect teeth can be made absolutely perfect. You tell him."

I nodded and went into my office. Cary Grant and Gunther were deep in conversation, but they stopped and Grant said, "What is that man doing out there?"

"He had an ancestor who participated in the Spanish Inquisition," I said. "Shelly's been trying to live up to the family tradition since he got his dental degree."

"I'd say his ancestor would be proud of him," said Grant.

I moved around my desk, pushed the bag of tacos toward them, and sat.

"He thinks he can make your teeth perfect," I said.

"I've learned to live with imperfection," Grant said, pointing to a familiar mole on his cheek. "That way you don't tempt the gods."

"Avoiding hubris," said Gunther.

"Indeed," said Grant. "What's that smell?"

"Greasy tacos," I said. "Have a couple."

Grant reached for the bag and pulled out a taco. I did the same, dripping sauce across assorted notes and letters. Gunther declined the treat.

"Any more George Halls?" I asked Gunther. "Neither of the two you gave me is the one we're looking for."

Gunther, his feet nowhere near touching the floor, took his notebook from his jacket pocket, opened it, and said, "Pasadena, a Georges Halle." He spelled it. "I called him. He is, like me, Swiss. I am certain he is not the one you seek."

"I had my secretary check casting agents," said Grant. "She's still working on it. No George Hall so far."

"Our George may not be from around here," I said.

"No," said Grant, carefully approaching the taco so that no grease dripped on his jacket or trousers, "I think he is. I was looking for local people and that's what our Mr. Volkman promised to deliver."

"So," I said, "we have nothing but the three cards in Volkman's pocket."

"We can each take one or go together," I said. "But . . ."

"I'd be recognized," Grant said, finishing his first taco. "Funny, I've worked all my adult life and most of my childhood working on being recognized. Standing out in a crowd has its disadvantages."

"I know," said Gunther. "I have learned that one must stand the stares with dignity."

"No one ever gives me a second look," I said. "Part of my charm. I'll follow up on the cards. Meanwhile . . . "

"Hold on," Grant said, holding up a hand and opening his mouth to speak.

He was interrupted by a loud roar from beyond the door. He looked at the door and back at me.

"I think our sleeping giant just woke up," Grant said.

The door to my office flew open and the giant stood there, looking at each one of us, his eyes stopping at Cary Grant as if he recognized but couldn't quite place him.

"Where is he?" asked the Mountain.

"He?" I asked.

"Dr. Minck," he said. "He pulled the wrong tooth. Now he's gone."

"Have a taco," I said, holding out the bag. Mountain took one and then slammed the door. If he intended, as I thought he did, to take on the Los Angeles Mangler, it wouldn't be much of a match.

"He stands out in a crowd," Grant said.

"So," I said. "Here's what I suggest we do."

Gunther and Grant looked at me.

"Volkman," I said, writing his name on an envelope on my desk. It was the back of a telephone bill I hadn't yet opened. "Gunther, can you? . . . "

"Just a minute," Grant said. "Have you got a photograph of this Volkman?"

I didn't, but I knew where to get one.

"It occurs to me," Grant continued, "that he might have been using a different name. If we can get a photograph we can show around. . . ."

"I'll get a photograph," I said.

I told them Volkman's address and said I'd take care of it.

"Almost four-thirty," Grant said, looking at his watch. "Gentlemen, it has been an interesting afternoon, but we've got to keep moving. You don't know how important it is to find George Hall and, if it still exists, the list of names Bruno Volkman was going to give me."

Grant got up, shook Gunther's hand, and looked at me as he reached for the door.

"Call my number any time," he said. "Say you're Sam Gronik of RKO. Find George Hall, Peters. A lot of lives may depend on it."

And he was gone.

Gunther and I looked at each other for a few seconds.

"I shall continue the search for George Hall," he said, climbing down from his chair.

"I'll follow up on the cards in Volkman's pocket and get a photograph of him," I said. "I'll call you at Mrs. Plaut's when I have something."

CHAPTER

I TURNED MY chair and looked out of the open window toward the Pacific Ocean. I couldn't see the ocean from my window, just the tops of buildings. Through a space between two other office buildings I could see traffic on Arapahoe Street. I was counting cars when my door opened and Violet came in.

Violet was trim, young, dark, and pretty, which was why Shelly had hired her. She was also smart.

"He wants to see you," she said.

"Shelly?"

She nodded.

"Tell him to come in."

"He's hiding. From that big guy whose tooth he pulled," she explained.

"Where is he?"

"Across the street at Tony's," she said. "He told me to close up and go home. So I'm closing up and going home."

"He really pull the wrong tooth?" I asked.

"You're asking me? I'd say it's six to four he did," said Violet.

I went over to Tony's, which was right across Hoover and about three doors to the left. Tony's has a couple of neon signs in the darkened window, one for Falstaff beer and the other for Gobel beer. The Falstaff sign had a flickering "r" that had been threatening for years to give up and turn the place into the Falstaff "Bee."

It was still early, so only the regulars and a handful of soldiers and sailors in uniform with nowhere else to go were at the small bar or talking at one of the tables. Tony's, which was owned by the Philoplis brothers—neither of whom was named Tony—served a good burger. Since I had given Mountain my last taco as a peace offering, I paused at the bar and ordered a burger and a beer while I looked around for Shelly.

I couldn't remember which Philopolis brother was Anton and which was Constantine. They didn't look much alike. One was tall and skinny with a sour face. The other was average height with some heft to him and a weary bartender smile that said he'd heard it all and expected to hear it again.

"Looking for the dentist?" asked the tall skinny one behind the bar.

"Yeah."

"Said you'd be here. All the way back in the last booth. I'll bring your burger and brew."

I headed for the back of Tony's and found Shelly scrunched up in the last booth on the right. He was wearing sunglasses and took them off when I sat down.

"It's me," I said.

"Thank God. He's going to kill me, Toby. You've got to do something." He cowered back into the corner of his side of the booth.

"Advice first," I said. "Take off the sunglasses. They're a lousy disguise and you're blind wearing them."

He squinted at me and in the general direction of the door to

Tony's. Then he reached into his pocket, took out his smudge-lensed regular glasses, and put them on.

"He tried to kill me," Shelly said, reaching for the half-full glass of beer in front of him. "Look."

Shelly pulled down his collar. I didn't see anything but a frayed shirt.

"What?"

"The marks. He tried to strangle me."

"If he tried, you'd be dead," I said.

"I managed to escape. He was still woozy from the gas or I would be a dead man. If I die, Toby, I want you to have everything. No, my sister should have everything. She's in Duluth. Violet can give you her address. But Mildred gets nothing. Promise me."

"That Mildred gets nothing or your sister gets all your rusting tools and the dental chair?"

"Both."

"I'll do my best."

Shelly wasn't looking at me during all this. His eyes were fixed on the door.

"Talk to Jeremy," he said. "Maybe Jeremy can reason with him. Or maybe I should just pack a bag and move."

"To Duluth?"

"San Diego," Shelly said. "Change my name and start a new practice. I've got a cousin in San Diego."

"You pulled the wrong tooth, Shel?"

He shrugged and looked at me.

"I could have sworn," he said. "It was big and yellow and right where he said the pain was. We all make mistakes."

"It's best not to make them with four-hundred-pound wrestlers with a bad temper," I said.

"I don't need Chinese sayings," he said. "I need protection. You owe me, Toby."

The skinny Philopolis brother brought my beer and burger, and Shelly said he'd like a burger too. Skinny Philopolis nodded and moved away.

"You want to hire me to protect you from Mountain?"

"Well, I was thinking more like you'd do it as an act of friendship," he said, leaning toward me and twitching his nose to keep his glasses from slipping off.

"How do I stop him?" I asked.

"You're the professional," Shelly said with a touch of exasperation. "Reason with him. Tell him I'm suffering from a rare disease, that I'm dying and my mind is going. Shoot him."

"I'll ask Jeremy to talk to him," I said.

"You think he knows where I live?"

Shelly had lived in a hotel since his wife Mildred had thrown him out. He was waiting for a divorce. Maybe his mind was going.

"I don't see how he can," I said.

"Maybe he tortured Violet, made her tell," he said, pushing back his eyeglasses and blinking at me through thick lenses."

"Violet is fine. She can take care of herself. She wouldn't turn you over."

"You think her husband Rocky will kill me when he gets back from the war? I mean I only touched her once and that was. . . ."

"Everyone is not trying to kill you, Shel," I said. "Mountain probably doesn't even want to kill you. Maybe he just wants his tooth back."

Shelly fumbled in his pocket and came up with the tooth. It was big and clean. He handed it to me.

"Give it back to him. Tell him he can have free dental care for the rest of his life."

"I don't think he'll take you up on that one," I said, pocketing the tooth.

"What did I do to deserve this?" he moaned.

I could have given him a long list, but I just ate my burger and drank my beer.

Ten minutes later, I left Shelly in the booth, eating his burger and feeling sorry for himself. I promised to talk to Jeremy and give Shelly a call later.

"I'll owe you, Toby," he had said as I got up to leave.

"You can pay me in cash," I said. When he opened his mouth to protest, I said, "This one is on the house. You pay for the beer and burger."

I went back across the street to the Farraday and took the elevator up to the seventh floor. People were coming out of offices, the workday over. Some were going down the stairs. Others were waiting for the elevator. The Farraday lobby echoed with talk and footsteps. When the elevator finally hit the seventh floor and opened, Jeremy was standing there with Natasha in his big arms. His daughter smiled at me. She could walk now, but just barely. Her favorite position was in her father's or mother's arms.

"We're going for a walk," he said.

Natasha reached out a hand to me and I touched it. Jeremy is huge, bald, and only beautiful when you get to know him. His wife, Alice, bore a strong resemblance to Marie Dressler. Natasha, on the other hand, was a striking, curly-haired kid with a huge smile.

"I was looking for you," I said.

He got in and I hit the button as he closed the elevator doors. The elevator made its usual little jerk and then started slowly downward.

"William Gorman," he said as Natasha became serious and poked her father's nose.

"Who?" I asked.

"Mountain Gorman," he said. "He came to see me after Dr. Minck removed the tooth. I had warned William against Dr. Minck, but he did not heed my advice. I attempted to reason with him, told him that a single tooth was meaningless and that I would gladly have one of my own removed to show him my sympathy. However, his bad tooth still hurts. He wants it out."

"He doesn't want Shelly to do it, does he?"

"He insists, in fact," said Jeremy. "I attempted to dissuade him, but to no avail."

Natasha squeezed her father's nose. He didn't seem to notice.

"William's reasoning is that Dr. Minck wouldn't dare make another error."

I couldn't imagine Shelly holding his hand steady enough to go back into Mountain's mouth with the pliers, but other than moving to San Diego and changing his name, he had little choice.

"Can you reach William?" I asked.

"Yes."

"Have him in Shelly's office at nine tomorrow morning," I said as the elevator moved jerkily downward.

"I can do that," he said. "The war is coming to a close, Toby."

"Looks that way," I said.

"We'll have to invade Japan," he said sadly while Natasha pulled at his left cheek. "Many people will die."

I didn't know what to say, so I shut up as the elevator came to a stop on the ground floor and Jeremy opened the door.

"One tooth, whether it's yours, mine or William's, carries little meaning," he said. "I think I'll write a poem about that."

"Sounds like a good idea," I said, grinning at Natasha.

My grin frightened most kids, but not Natasha. She gave me a wave and I hurried across the lobby and through the Farraday door, ignoring the voice of Juanita somewhere on the stairs behind me. I was having trouble dealing with the present, had never done well facing the past, and had no interest in knowing the future.

Shelly was in the same booth, his sunglasses back on, still nursing a beer. I sat again.

"Who?" he said with a start.

"Me again, Shel. Will you take those things off?"

He took the sunglasses off again and put his eyeglasses on. They were even more smudged than they had been before.

"Is he out there?" he asked, peering toward the door.

"No, Shel," I said. "Jeremy's taken care of it. Tomorrow morning at nine, Mountain will be in your office. He wants you to take out the right tooth. He will not kill you. He won't even hurt you. He may even pay you."

Shelly looked terrified.

"I can't go back in that mouth," he said. "It's a trick. As soon as I put my fingers in there, he'll bite them off and my career is over. I'll have to wear white gloves filled with cotton and people will think I'm weird."

"How could anyone think you're weird, Sheldon?" I asked. "Tomorrow at nine. Be there. Do it right."

"My hands will shake," he said, holding out his hands to show they were already shaking.

"Take something to steady them," I said.

"I won't be able to sleep tonight," he said, moving his head slowly from side to side.

"Small price to pay," I said.

"I guess," he said.

I left him there and made a decision. It was still light. I had planned to wait till dark, but it didn't make much difference. If the police were watching Volkman's apartment, they'd be there all day and all night. I didn't think the police had the time or manpower to watch a dead man's apartment twenty-four hours a day or even a few hours a day. And I doubted if the people who had arranged for me to get caught in the apartment with Volkman's body were watching the place.

I got in my car and headed for Volkman's. The only reason I spotted the Buick following me was that I pulled into a Texaco station on Pico for gas and glanced at my rearview mirror just as the Buick came to a stop at the curb.

I stayed in the car while the attendant filled the tank. I adjusted my mirror so I could see the Buick. There were two people inside it. I couldn't see them clearly. They were leaning back into the early evening shadow.

When I pulled out of the gas station, I drove slowly, turning left at the first corner, away from the direction I had been going in. I kept going slowly, letting the Buick keep up with me half a block back. I couldn't outrun the Buick, and I didn't want to let the driver know I'd spotted him if I could help it.

I made another slow left, leaving the Buick out of sight for a few seconds. I hit the gas pedal and looked around. I saw a narrow driveway on my right, checked my rearview mirror, and skidded into the driveway. There was a small garage on my right. I pulled onto the lawn behind it so that my car couldn't be seen from the street. I got out, climbed over a fence into the backyard of the house next door, and crouched behind some bushes with little red berries.

The Buick came slowly down the street. I watched as whoever was inside the car checked out the houses and driveways. When the car passed the house, I moved around the bushes and watched it get to the corner and stop. The two people were trying to decide which way to turn. They went left. They might come back. I turned to go back to my car and found myself facing a bulky old man wearing a USC sweatshirt and a baseball cap.

"What the hell are you doin'?" he demanded.

"Inspection," I said. "Los Angeles County Insect and Vermin Control Department. Report of Sacker weevils in this neighborhood."

"Sacker weevils?" he asked with a look that said I neither resembled a government inspector nor that he believed in Sacker weevils any more than he believed in the tooth fairy, who had long before absconded with any teeth the man had once possessed. He had, however, a fine set of dentures.

"New, worked their way up from Mexico," I explained, leaning over to examine the bush I was standing next to.

"Bugs are always coming up from Mexico and Texas," he said. "I use the Flit can, spray the hell out of everything, but you got to stay ahead of the goddamn bugs."

"I agree," I said, standing. "Well, your yard looks clear."

"Good," he said. "I'll get out the Flit."

"Stay ahead of them," I said, moving toward the fence.

"Where are you going?" he asked.

"Checking the neighbors," I said. "Every one, up and down the block."

"What do they look like?" he asked.

"Your neighbors?"

"The damn bugs," he snapped.

"Like watermelon seeds with legs," I said.

With that I went over the fence and headed for my Crosley. I had lost time talking to the old man. I moved fast, leaving a wake of destruction in the grass and the small tomato patch in the yard where I had parked. I should have left some money in an envelope or my name and phone number, but I didn't have time. I would just have to add that to a long list of minor guilts I'd accumulated in a lifetime of bad decisions.

I pulled back out onto the street, looking in the direction the Buick had turned. There were a few cars moving, but no Buick. I drove back the way I had first come, made a left, and kept going for five blocks before I turned left again and made a circle that took me half a block from Volkman's apartment.

There were two Buicks parked on the street, neither one of which was the one that had followed me. I made my way back up the stairs to Volkman's apartment. There was nothing to indicate that a dead man had been found inside. All was quiet. Birds chirped. Somewhere dishes rattled. I tried the door. It was locked. Getting it open was no problem.

Inside, I moved quickly across the living room to the bedroom and went to the dresser. The photograph of the little boy and the woman was still there. The picture of Volkman and the other man wasn't.

"Looking for this?" a voice said.

I turned fast, hoping a good lie would come, but I didn't need one. Cary Grant stepped out of the closet, the same closet where I'd found Volkman's body. The framed photograph was in his hand.

"You gave me the address," he said. "I thought about it for a while and decided that I couldn't let you take all the risks. You're helping, but the problem is mine."

"I think you should get out of here," I said, reaching for the photograph.

"I think you're right," he said. "By the way, which one of these men is Volkman?"

"On the left."

"Yes, I think I recognize him," Grant said, examining the photograph. "From Paramount. But the other man. Him I definitely recognize. Victor Cookinham."

"Victor Cookinham?"

"Can't forget a name like that, can you?" Grant said. "Cookinham's an agent."

"Talent?" I asked.

"For the German government," he said. "He's been missing for almost two years. Just managed to get away when the FBI was closing in on him."

"How do you? . . . " I began but we heard the front door open.

Not again, I thought. At this rate, I'd be paying back Marty Leib for the rest of whatever remained of my life. Grant moved to the partially closed bedroom door and peeked into the living room. Then he turned to me and whispered, "Let me."

With that, he stepped into the living room with me right behind him.

A man wearing a flannel shirt and trousers with suspenders stood there. Grant stopped suddenly, a look of indignation and surprise on his face.

"Who are you and what are you doing here?" the actor demanded.

"Who am . . . I'm the janitor," the man said. "The Sullivans downstairs said they heard. . . ."

"The Sullivans? Never heard of them," Grant said, looking at me. "You?"

"Never heard of them," I agreed.

"Well, anyway, with Mr. Volkman being . . . you know what happened . . . I," the janitor stammered.

"This man is Bruno's second cousin," Grant said, putting an arm around my shoulder. "The deceased's only living relative."

"Only living . . . I thought he had . . . " the janitor tried.

"Dead," said Grant. "All dead. Only Mr. Beeberhoffer is left."

"I'm sorry to. . . ."

"Sorry is the perfect word," said Grant gently. "Mr. Beeberhoffer is going to take care of all the funeral arrangements. We just came by to pick up a few family mementos."

Grant held out the photograph for the janitor.

"Remarkable likeness," the actor said, reexamining the photograph. Remarkable."

"Looks very much like him, but. . . ."

"You'd be doing Mr. Beeberhoffer a great favor if you'd sell the furniture," Grant said. "Of course, you could keep whatever little it brings in. It would be a great favor."

"I'd be happy. . . ."

"Good," said Grant with a smile. "I could tell I could count on you the second I saw you, Mr.? . . . "

"Stepple, Amos Stepple. May I say something?"

"By all means, Mr. Stepple," said Grant.

"Who are you?"

"Friend of the family," Grant said. "Trained in grief counseling in the Dutch army. As you can see, Mr. Beeberhoffer is so overcome with grief he can't even speak."

"I see that, but. . . ."

"Take the money you get for the furniture and buy something nice for your wife and children," Grant said, ushering the janitor to the front door."

"I don't have any . . . I mean my wife has two daughters from her first marriage, but they're in Seattle and. . . ."

"No need to explain," Grant said, opening the door. "I can tell your heart's in the right place."

The man put a hand to his chest and looked at me, completely baffled.

"We'll be going ourselves in just a few minutes," said Grant. "We'll be quiet. Mr. Beeberhoffer just wants to sit for a bit, begin to accept his loss. You understand."

"Not really," said the janitor, "but I can keep whatever I sell the furniture for?"

Grant looked at me and I nodded. Then Grant closed the door on the bewildered man.

"Anything else we need here?" he asked.

"No," I said, then changed my mind. "Yes. Maybe. In the bottom drawer of the dresser if the cops didn't take them."

We moved into the bedroom again, and I opened the bottom drawer and pushed the underwear aside. The Nazi literature was still there. Grant scooped it up and said, "Let's get out of here before Mr. Stepple decides to call the police."

We went out the front door and down the stairs.

"Where's your car?" I asked.

"There," he said, pointing at a dark DeSoto at the curb.

"I was followed when I left my office," I said as we walked. "Dark Buick. Two men. They might show up here."

"Then let's not be here," said Grant, handing me the photograph and the Nazi literature. "Call me later."

I said I would and watched while he got into his car and drove away. I looked both ways. No Buick. I was back in my Crosley, thinking of what to do next and listening to Bill Stern the Colgate shave cream man telling me that Gunder Haegg, the Swedish long-distance runner, had decided he had reached his peak and was considering retirement. Stern sounded very sad.

I switched the radio to *Blondie* and heard Arthur Lake as Dagwood trying to explain to Mr. Dithers, his boss, why he needed a raise to pay for a new roof. Everyone was having problems.

CHAPTER 9

IT WAS TOO late to do anything more that day, so I headed for Mrs. Plaut's boardinghouse. There were a few parking spaces. I took the one closest to the house and walked up the short concrete path to the steps, the photo and literature tucked under my arm.

When I entered the house, Mrs. Plaut was standing there.

"You are back," she said, as if I had been among the missing.

"I am back," I said.

"There's an egg salad sandwich on Holsum bread on the table in your room."

"Thank you."

I moved toward the stairs.

"A Buick, green, has been driving past my house for the past hour," she said. "A man has been looking at my house from inside the Buick. Such things have occurred before and usually in some connection to you. Is this one of those things, Mr. Peelers?"

"It may be," I said.

"You lead a life of books, nooks, and crannies," she said. "Is it in your capacity as an exterminator or an editor that these men are seeking you?"

"Could be either," I said, moving toward the stairs.

"Shall I call the police?"

"No. I'll take care of it."

"Are they dangerous?"

"Maybe."

"If they come to the door and try to get in without my permission, I may have to shoot them with the Mister's shotgun," she said seriously.

"I wouldn't grieve," I said. "Unless they're policemen, which is a distinct possibility."

"I would not want to shoot policemen," she said. "I'll simply hold them at bay and call you."

"That would be best," I said.

I had complete confidence in Mrs. Plaut and was sure she would do exactly as she said. If not, two bad guys, or possibly good ones, would get themselves shot. I was well up the stairs when she said, "The manuscript is resting comfortably next to your plate with the egg salad sandwich on Holsum bread."

Resting comfortably. That's what they said at the hospital when you called about a sick friend or relative and they didn't want to tell you that things had not gone nearly as well as they would have liked.

"I'll read it tonight," I said.

I heard Mrs. Plaut lock the front door and then go into her rooms as I hit the second-floor landing and made my way to my room.

When I turned on the light, I saw Dash curled up on the couch against the wall. He looked up at me without moving his head and closed his eyes again.

I took off my jacket, hung it up, kicked off my shoes, and moved to the refrigerator, where I took out the milk and poured myself a glass of milk and a bowlful for Dash. He didn't come running across the floor to drink it. I'd need more milk in a day or two. I took a couple of Doc Parry's pills and three aspirin.

The egg salad sandwich was just what I needed. Lots of mayo, thick with eggs, pepper, and salt with a slice of onion on top. Fuel for the task ahead.

I picked up Mrs. Plaut's manuscript and began to read as I kept eating:

THE SORENSON TWINS IN NEW ORLEANS

New Orleans is a city of humidity, noise, music, sin, and seafood you have to get to by cracking lots of shells which is fine with some people but is not for me.

The Sorenson twins, who were on my mother's side, were named Sidney and Parker. They were boys of a devious nature and the time was 1814 or somewhere nearby. Andrew Jackson had broken Sidney's foot during the war when the general in a hurry to get to the outhouse on the Kelsy Plantation stepped on him and just kept going without an I'm sorry. There were bowel problems during that war and even a great general with bad manners was not immune which was the only satisfaction Sidney could take from the incident.

Sidney and Parker opened the Sorenson Tavern with money they had taken from their father Abel. They had taken the money back in Ohio considering it due to them because they had worked the family farm for twenty years or more without a thank you or a nickel. So while I do not condone their theft, I grant them some understanding.

Then the ptomaine, if that's what it was, and the great fight.

Parker was the cook. Sidney limped around greeting and serving people. Sometimes, but not often, they switched places, but though they were twins they didn't fool anyone, not that they were trying to, because you see Sidney had this limp given him by General Jackson. Now Parker could have pretended to limp but that would not have been in good taste and what would the point have been? Folly.

When the ptomaine and battle took place, the Sorenson twins were two weeks from celebrating their fortieth birthday. The night of the disaster they were serving dinner to a full house, all tables taken, shells crunching on the wooden floor, people slurping shrimp, clams, lobsters, and here and there a fried fish.

Through the wooden door came three men wearing dark fur coats and carrying muzzle-loading Pennsylvania long rifles and wearing big hats and sporting unkempt beards and looking mean and out for trouble.

This was not an unusual sight in the Sorenson Tavern, which had an unruly reputation, but when Sidney told them they would have to wait a few minutes for a table, the three men took umbrage and shot a quartet consisting of a gambler, a thief, a prostitute, and a man named Davies who may or may not have been a whiskey drummer.

There were four dead and a rash of pandemonium. People scurried and the three men with long guns sat at the table which was no longer occupied by the living.

What next transpired is a confusing mess.

To start with the dog appeared. He was a big dog. He had all his teeth and a temper. Parker later claimed that the animal did not belong to him or to Sidney. Nonetheless, the dog attacked the three men in coats carrying long guns. When he, or maybe it was a she, attacked the first man whose fingers were wet with oyster drippings, the second one from only feet away fired his long gun. The shot missed the dog and all but the man with the wet fingers. The shot killed him dead which led the other man at the table to shoot the man who had just shot the other man if you follow my meaning. I imagine the first dead man bore a kinship to the now only remaining intruder. The dog looked around confused and attacked the last living man at the table who fired hitting Sidney in his already- Andrew Jackson–maimed foot.

The last man of the three fled screaming, "Mercy on me. Mercy damn." He was out of the door and gone.

Sidney lost his foot and for the remainder of his life walked with a special shoe. The dog ate some oysters and disappeared. The militia constable declared that everyone killed everyone and left the tavern ordering the Sorenson twins to see to the burial.

A grim and grisly tale but one not ended.

Sick at heart the twins sold their tavern parted ways and moved West where Sidney became Limping Sid Lightning, gunfighter, and Parker became the Reverend Sorenson in Tucson where he spawned many a child and was known for his sermons on the wonders of dogs and the joys of cooking.

Amen.

That ended the chapter. I was beginning to notice something in Mrs. Plaut's chapters. People were always getting shot or going mad. There lay a sadistic streak in Mrs. Irene Plaut, and I decided, for a change, to suggest something. Why shouldn't the next chapter she wrote be about something pleasant?

I talked to Dash for a while and looked at Volkman's business cards, trying to decide where to start.

"School of Performance," I said to Dash. "Maybe Volkman had the acting bug."

Dash looked at the wall as if he were thinking.

"A typewriter repair man," I went on. "I didn't see a typewriter in Volkman's apartment."

Dash walked slowly toward the window.

"A radio salesman," I said, flipping to the last card. "I don't remember a radio either."

Dash leaped to the window ledge and jumped out to the branch of the nearby tree.

With no one now to talk to and my neck and head still aching, I decided to go to bed early.

As soon as I was asleep, Koko the Clown entered my dream world, his face just inches away as he said, "Cincinnati." I must have groaned in my sleep.

Koko shrugged and pulled his head back. I was in Cincinnati. Don't ask me how I know it's Cincinnati. I've never been there, but I was sure it was. I started walking, looking at doors, stopping to knock at a few. No one answered. There were no cars in Cincinnati. No people. I was afraid because I knew where I'm going. The bridge. I crossed it to the island, which had more houses. This time I was sure if I knocked at the right one, someone or something would answer and I wouldn't be happy. I stopped at a white door, lifted my hand to knock, knowing this was the place. Before I could knock, someone else knocked and I woke up.

"Seven-thirty in the A.M.," said Mrs. Plaut. "Breakfast is a surprise."

"I hate surprises," I said, sitting up, drenched in sweat, a knot of pain in my neck.

"This one is special. Did you read my chapter?"

"I did," I said, sitting up, blinking, and rubbing my neck.

"And?"

"A lot of people get killed," I said.

"Yes. That's what happened."

"Are there going to be any chapters in the book where none of your relatives get killed, kill someone else, or go crazy?"

"I don't think so," she said. "Except the chapter on Miss Polly True, my grandmother's aunt."

"Write that one next," I said, but I had little hope.

She disappeared into the hall, leaving the door open.

I went through my morning ritual of shaving and showering, then searched my closet for something to wear. I really needed to get to the cleaners. I put on the same pants I'd worn the day before and a white shirt I knew was at least a size too large. I downed two Doc Parry pills and two aspirin and told myself I was ready for the day.

Mrs. Plaut would not reveal the contents of her breakfast surprise. It was square, about an inch thick, brown on the top, and not too firm. We all tried it and looked at each other. It was good, but one likes to know what one is eating.

"Very good," said Ben Bidwell. "Tastes like an egg souffle."

"It contains no eggs," Mrs. Plaut said.

"Flour," Emma Simcox tried.

"None," said Mrs. Plaut.

"Meat," I said.

"Not exactly."

What is "not exactly" meat? I decided I didn't want to know. I finished my surprise and excused myself.

"After termites?" Mrs. Plaut asked.

"Not exactly," I said, moving to Mrs. Plaut's living room and then into the hall with Gunther a few steps behind me. I stopped and looked down at him.

"Three more George Halls," he said. "One in San Gabriel. One in Whittier. One in Long Beach. I have their addresses."

"I'll check on them tomorrow," I said.

"There is a likelihood this George Hall is a Nazi or a collaborator with the Nazis?" Gunther said.

"A likelihood," I agreed.

"Then I should like to join in the pursuit. I should like to go to these George Halls to attempt to discover if they are guilty."

"Okay," I said. "But be careful. Wait. How about taking Jeremy with you?"

"I should be delighted to have his company," said Gunther.

So, up the stairs I went and called Jeremy. I hoped Alice wouldn't answer the phone. I represented danger to her husband, but the few times I had excluded him from a case where I needed him, he made it clear in subtle ways that he felt I thought he was too old at sixty-plus or too domesticated. In fact, it would be good to have Jeremy around to protect Gunther if he found himself in trouble.

Jeremy readily agreed to help when I told him we were probably dealing with Nazi spies. I told him Gunther would pick him up in half an hour in front of the Farraday.

"Be careful," I called to Gunther as I went down the stairs.

"And you too," he said.

No green Buick followed me as I headed up Tujunga on my way to Burbank. This time it was a dark blue Plymouth. Whoever was on my tail had a choice of transportation. When I came to a light at Magnolia and Verdugo, I checked for my .38 in the glove compartment. It was there. I took it out and tucked it in my pocket. Before the light changed, I checked my rearview mirror for the blue Plymouth. It was there, two cars back. The two men inside were wearing hats, the brims pulled forward, so I couldn't see much of their faces. The passenger looked big. The driver looked average.

On a good day I probably wouldn't have been able to take them on without a weapon, and today wasn't one of my better ones. My shoulder was sore. My neck was feeling a little better and my head no longer hurt, but it wouldn't take much to send me back to the emergency room.

Caroll College was on the north end of Mariposa Street. I knew the place from my days as a Burbank patrolman. It was a small campus, ten buildings, all two-story brick except for the administration building, which was five stories. The buildings had gone up at different times and were plunked down in no particular order. They looked pretty much the same, as if some weary administrators had just pulled out the well-worn plans every time they came up with enough money to put up another building.

I parked in the lot in a space reserved for visitors. Most of the spaces were taken. I got out and headed toward the campus on a concrete path. People who appeared to be students and faculty were moving slowly ahead of and behind me.

I asked two girls with almost identical curly blonde hair and big smiles where the School of Performance was. They told me to follow them and, when we went past the administration building, one of the girls shaded her eyes and then pointed north.

"That one," she said. "It's over there."

"Thanks," I said and looked back toward the parking lot. I didn't see the two men from the Plymouth, but I knew they were around.

The building I headed for was nothing special. Red brick that needed blasting. Vines covering the front of the building and around the windows. January green. It looked like a college building.

Inside, the hall was dark. Voices and footsteps echoed, not quick and deep silver like at the Farraday but baritone and serious. I sidestepped a pair of students, each with an armful of books, and went through the door on my right marked "Office."

There were three desks in the room, one facing the door and me. Two of the desks were empty. A solid woman in her fifties at the desk facing the door looked up at me through her glasses.

"Can I help you?" she asked.

She had a pencil in her right hand and began tapping the point on her blotter. The pencil wanted to get back to work.

"I'm looking for Jacklyn Wright," I said.

"You have an appointment with Professor Wright?"

"Do I need one?"

"It's best."

"Sometimes we can't do what's best," I said.

"She has a class in the theater," the woman said, pencil now tapping impatiently faster.

"When will it be over?" I asked.

"I'm afraid . . . "

"Don't be," I said. "My name is Herman Bubinsky, executive producer at Universal Studios."

She stopped tapping. I had her attention now.

"I understand from a source I can't divulge that there are two very promising young actors in the program whom I should take a look at."

"Yes," she said. "There are a number of very promising students. Your source must have seen our production of *The Importance of Being Ernest.*"

"Exactly," I said with a smile.

She looked at me again. Producers came in all kinds of packages. I knew one at Republic named Smidruth, Andrew Smidruth. He looked like a starving ghost and mumbled, but he produced over one hundred Westerns with people like Bob Steele, Tim Holt, Tom Tyler, and even a couple with Tim McCoy and Buck Jones. No Andrew Smidruth movie had ever lost a dime. And then there was Oliver Cartt, whose real name was Cartohomovich. He had an accent so thick you could drown in it. And he was an overweight slob who dressed like a bum. Oliver Cartt slave-drove a small crew at Monogram into almost fifty movies a year, none taking more than five days to shoot. He worked Bobby Breen into exhaustion and got Frankie Darrow and Mantan Moreland so confused they didn't know what picture they were working on.

"The theater is down the hall to your left," the woman said, putting down her pencil. "The class will be over in a few minutes.

I'm sure Professor Wright won't mind if you stop in and introduce yourself."

"Thank you," I said.

"Would you like to leave a card?" she asked.

"I would," I said, "but I don't think I'm ready to officially introduce myself until I've had a chance to talk to Professor Wright. You understand."

"Perfectly," the woman said.

Which was good, because I had no idea what I was talking about.

"I was an actress," she said as I started to turn for the door.

"Really?"

"Character roles," she said. "Silent pictures. Did two Garbos and a Harold Lloyd."

"Treasure the memories," I said.

"I nearly starved," the woman said. She handed me a thin brochure on the School of Performance and went back to whatever she was working on.

I pocketed the brochure and went out the door. I had no trouble finding the theater. First, it was clearly marked Gardner Theater. Second, the voices of people acting came through the double doors next to a barred box-office window. The actors were projecting, speaking clearly, not sounding like real people.

I opened one of the doors carefully, stepped in, and closed it behind me. The theater was small, about two hundred seats, and the house was dark except for the lights on the stage. I stood in the rear next to the door in the darkness.

Two young men and two young women were on the stage. One of the young women—skinny, pretty, long hair, looking a bit confused—was the only one holding a script. There was a sofa and two plain wooden chairs on the stage. About fifteen students sat in the first two rows of the audience.

A woman with, dark blonde hair tied back with a red ribbon,

and wearing dark slacks and a loose-fitting blouse stood in front of the stage, looking up with her arms folded.

"Ellen," the woman said. "You've got the lines down. Your projection is fine. Your diction impeccable. Your emotion nonexistent."

Someone in the audience giggled.

"Ellen," the woman went on, "there are lots of ways to act. You can pretend you're the person, pretend so well that for the duration of the performance you believe it, you live it. You can also become the person, forget that you are even performing, let the character do Ellen. Draw on who you are."

"Yes," said Ellen meekly.

"How many times have I told all of you this?"

"Thirty-six," a young man in the first row said.

"Eighteen," came a girl's voice in the second row.

The woman in the billowy blouse turned to her class and smiled.

"The number of times doesn't matter," she said. "It's like psychotherapy. You can hear it a dozen times, a hundred times and know it's true, but until you feel it, nothing changes. Questions? No? Good. Lawrence, try your lines again. Ellen, remember when you get your cue, come right in the second Lawrence finishes. No, overlap his last word. You're bursting to speak. Let's try it."

The young man named Lawrence brushed a lock of straight dark hair from his eyes, adjusted the blue and red sweater vest he wore over a white shirt, and folded his arms as he said, "Believe you? Why should I believe you? When have you ever, ever told me the truth? Believe you? I'd be more likely to believe the German War Ministry."

The girl with the script jumped in, her voice a slight tremble that might have been acting but was probably fear.

"Michael," she said, "I had no choice. My father. My God, Michael, I told you what happened to my father."

She looked at her script.

"If I had told you . . ."

"If you had trusted me," he said.

"Enough," called the woman in the billowy blouse. "Ellen, you didn't overlap. You paused, waiting for the cue line. And, at this point, you really should have your lines down. You don't need the script. You're using it as a crutch."

The woman checked her watch.

"It's almost time," she said. "Back here at three. That means everybody."

The four students on the stage said a few words to each other as those in the front row moved past me talking as they went out the door. I didn't move and no one seemed to see me.

When they were gone, the woman I assumed was Jacklyn Wright remained in front of the stage, pencil in hand, writing something.

I moved out of the shadows and started down the aisle trying to be quiet.

"Yes?" she said without turning her head, without pausing in what she was writing.

"Professor Wright?" I asked.

She turned and faced me, her arms again folded across her chest.

"Yes."

As I came closer, I could see that she was older than I had thought, certainly in her forties. Her skin was smooth and her face almost pretty, but on it there was that look of experience that comes with the bumps you never quite get used to and try to protect yourself from.

I moved in front of her.

"I was watching from in back," I said.

"And you spotted the next Tyrone Power," she said wearily. "You are?"

"Name is Toby Peters," I said. "I'm looking for someone but not another Tyrone Power. A man named Bruno Volkman."

She pursed her lips, thought for a few seconds and said, "Name doesn't ring a bell. Why are you looking for him?"

"I'm not at liberty to say, but it's important."

I took out my wallet and showed her my investigator's license. She actually read it. Nobody reads them. Then she looked up.

"I have a photograph," I said.

I took the photo out of my pocket and handed it to her. She nodded her head in recognition.

"This one I don't know," she said, pointing at Victor Cookinham. "The other one is Martin Adams."

She handed the photograph back to me and I pocketed it.

"How do you know Martin Adams?" I asked.

She reached for a large dark purse on the stage behind her, pulled out a package of Old Golds, and lit one while she thought.

"I do two night classes once a week, three hours, right here, for telephone operators, salesmen, housewives, shopkeepers, jewelers, lawyers, doctors. You name it. They've all been told by someone, maybe themselves, that they can act. One class is for beginners, the other for more advanced students."

"And Martin Adams was in one of your classes?"

"Still is. We meet on Tuesday nights."

"He won't make it," I said. "He took two bullets in the back in Elysian Park two nights ago."

She shook her head, smoked, blew smoke in the air and said, "Robbery?"

"In a way," I said.

"No real talent, but learned his lines," she said. "The accent might have gotten him some bit roles, Nazi soldiers, waiters, but nothing more than that. He wanted to get rid of the accent."

"But he was in your advanced class?" I asked.

She shrugged and said, "Advanced is a relative term. Let's say he was in on the fringe. We're not talking about Laurence Olivier and Greer Garson here, Mr. Peters."

"What did he say he did for a living?"

"First day in class each student gets onstage alone and has fifteen minutes to tell his or her life story. Martin Adams had a very interesting one. Escaped from Germany. Dangerous assignments for the government. He made it all up. That was all right. The purpose wasn't to find out the truth but to see how he carried himself onstage. As I said, he was about average."

"You told him?"

"I told him he shouldn't have high hopes, that the competition was enormous, that he'd have to face a lot of disappointments. He said he had friends in the movie business who would give him a hand."

"You believed him?"

She took a drag on her cigarette and shrugged.

"I think he believed himself," she said. "How did you know he came here?"

"This was in his wallet when he died."

I handed her the card with her name on it. She glanced at it and handed it back.

"Was he friendly with anyone else in the class?" I asked.

She shook her head "no" and looked at her cigarette.

"No, he came early, kept to himself, and was always the first one out the door."

"No talent," I said.

"Not enough. When the bug bites, it digs deep. I tell my students on the first day that they'll know one of three things when they finish the course. They'll know they have the talent and determination to try. They'll know they have no talent and should give it up and spend their free time on something that they can do.

Or they'll be insane enough to keep going even if they can't act. I've had a few with no talent at all who actually wound up making some kind of living in the business. Mad determination can sometimes carry you a long way."

"And you?"

"I had some talent," she said. "My looks were passable, but the camera didn't love me, didn't even notice me. I could give you a list of B-movies I was in, a few featured roles, but you wouldn't remember me even if you remembered the pictures."

"But you're a good teacher?"

"A damn good teacher," she said. "I tell the truth, and the truth sets them free or sends them crying. Crying today beats crying tomorrow. You ever do any acting?"

"In my job? All the time, but mostly I play myself."

"That's not always easy."

"I've had a lot of practice," I said. "What else can you tell me about Martin Adams?"

The door closed behind me. My back was to it. Jacklyn Wright looked over my shoulder and I turned. The door closed. I didn't see who had been there, but I had a pretty good idea.

"That's about it," she said.

"Last question, did Adams ever mention or have you ever heard of a man named George Hall?"

"George Hall," she repeated. "I don't think so. I've had a lot of students over the past ten years. There might have been a George Hall, but I think I would have remembered. I'm sorry. Did this George Hall kill Martin?"

"I don't know," I said.

I held out my hand. We shook. She had a firm grip, plus confidence and toughness. But then again, it might have been an act.

"Well," I said. "Thanks."

I went up the aisle and opened the door half expecting to see the two guys from the Plymouth. They had probably heard some of my conversation with Jacklyn Wright. I didn't know how much. It didn't matter. I hadn't learned anything.

There weren't many people on the campus. Classes were in session. I walked slowly. Even more slowly when I turned the corner by the administration building and saw the two men who had been following me standing next to my car.

I could have turned and ran, but I had a feeling that even if my neck and shoulder didn't throb and my head didn't threaten to ache, I had no chance of outrunning them. So, I walked up to my car.

The bigger one was clean shaven, with a nice blue suit, almost matching hat, tie, in his late thirties. The shorter one was a duplicate of his partner, with a slightly brighter tie.

My right hand was on the gun in my pocket.

"Mr. Peters," the shorter man said, looking at my right hand. "You won't be needing that."

He took his wallet out of his pocket and held it open.

I stepped forward to look. The card identified him as Agent Louis D'Argentero, Federal Bureau of Investigation. The bigger one started to reach for his wallet. I told him it wasn't necessary.

"Mr. Peters," the bigger one said. "We think you've gotten yourself involved in something that involves national security."

I said nothing.

"You were present when a man named Bruno Volkman was murdered," his partner said. "Volkman has been under scrutiny for some time because of his associations with suspected Nazi sympathizers."

"Like Victor Cookinham?" I asked.

"Victor Cookinham is Hans Vogel," said the big guy. "Former professor of history at the University of Hamburg. We've been trying to find him for weeks."

"You took a photograph of Vogel and Volkman from Volkman's apartment," said D'Argentero.

They had a good act, well balanced.

"You also took some Nazi propaganda," said the big one.

An older man with a briefcase who looked like a faculty member turned his head toward us as he moved across the parking lot. He decided to mind his own business and moved to a two-door Pontiac that needed a new paint job.

"What's your interest in this case?" asked D'Argentero.

"I have a client," I said. "I've been hired to try to find out who killed Volkman."

"Your client?"

"Can't tell you," I said. "But I can say my client is definitely not a spy."

Actually, I wasn't quite so sure about that, but if Grant was a spy, I was confident he was on our side even if the FBI knew nothing about it.

"I'm sorry, we can't simply take your word for that," said the big agent, whose name I hadn't been given.

"Then we're all sorry," I said.

"We can bring you in for questioning under Bureau wartime guidelines," said the big guy.

"I'm used to that."

"We know," said D'Argentero. "We'd prefer your cooperation. This is far trickier than you may be able to handle on your own, and even a small mistake could be very bad for our country."

I thought about it for a few seconds and made a decision.

"Give me two days," I said. "I'll talk to my client. Then I'll tell you what I know."

"We may not have two days," said the larger agent.

"Two days and you stop following me," I said.

They looked at each other.

"Two days," D'Argentero said. "Forty-eight hours from right now. Then, full cooperation."

"Thanks."

D'Argentero nodded and they moved across the lot toward the Plymouth.

I opened my car door, placed my pile of Nazi literature, the photograph of Volkman and Vogel, and the Caroll College brochure on the seat next to me, put my .38 back in the glove compartment, and sat there until their car had pulled out of the lot. Then I was on my way.

There was no point in trying to think. The only thing I could do was what I did best, blunder straight ahead. With this in mind, I headed for Jack Baron's Radios and Phonographs. I pulled out the card I had taken from Volkman's pocket and double-checked it for the address on La Cienega.

CHAPTER 10

BARON'S RADIOS AND PHONOGRAPHS was a two-window shop with an entrance between the windows. On one side of Baron's was M'Lady's Gifts and Greeting Cards. On the other side was a Chinese carry-out restaurant.

The windows of Baron's displayed a variety of radios, mostly tabletops, and a few phonographs. There was a Minute Man poster in the window ordering me to buy United States bonds and stamps and a poster of that RCA dog listening to the sound coming out of that big megaphone.

I went in. A little bell on the door announced me, but no one appeared. I walked over to one of the tables where some little radios sat. I was touching the smooth surface of one when a man came through an open door at the back of the shop.

He was slightly stoop-shouldered, had large round glasses, and wore a blue shirt with rolled-up sleeves. A pair of headsets hung around his neck.

"Yes sir," he said, blinking.

"Looking for a radio," I said. "Tabletop. Nothing expensive."

At that point, I realized I was actually in the market for a radio. Why not? I could see myself lying on my mattress, propped up with pillows, drinking a cup of coffee, listening to *I Love a Mystery*.

"Got your hand on a nice one," he said. "1939 FADA L-96W ivory Bakelite body, easy-to-read gold dials with gold numbers. Compact. Yours for eighteen dollars."

"Nice," I said, picking it up.

He plugged it in, turned it on, and searched for a station. He found *The Goldbergs*. "I'm warning you, Solomon," came the high-pitched voice. The audience laughed.

"Great sound, good balance," the salesman said.

He turned off the radio and pointed to the one next to it. "Another Bakelite. Zenith 6D-512. Dark brown. 1938. New tubes. Tuned it up myself. Also eighteen dollars."

"What I'm looking for, Mr. . . ."

"Baron, Jack Baron," he said, holding out his hand. We shook.

"What I'm looking for is something with a bigger sound."

"No trouble. Those four. All Philcos. I could give you the 80 model for twenty."

"Can I just look around?" I asked.

"Take your time. I've got a full line of Zeniths, Atwater Kents, Crosleys, American Bosch, Emerson. Good deals."

"Friend of mine recommended you," I said, touching an upright wooden Emerson that looked a little too big for the table in my room.

Baron smiled and nodded.

"Name is Bruno Volkman," I said, pretending to examine the Emerson but watching him for a reaction. He gave none.

"Doesn't ring a bell," Baron said.

I took out the photograph of Volkman and Cookinham and showed it to him.

"You carry photographs of your friends around with you?"

"He's sort of missing," I said.

Baron looked at the photograph again.

"Man with the beard, no. Other guy is Martin something. Martin Andrews, Martin Adams, something like that."

"He bought more than one radio from you?" I asked.

"Didn't buy any radios," Baron said. "Transcribers. Phonographs. Make records like they do on the radio. Bought one about four, five months ago and updated to a better model about four weeks ago. Follow me."

He walked back toward and through the door at the rear of the shop, with me a few steps behind.

We were in a cluttered room with shelves along both walls and a worktable in the middle filled with wires, tubes, turntables, and pieces of electrical machinery I didn't recognize. The shelves on one wall were filled with neatly stacked records in brown sleeves. The other wall held phonographs in various stages of repair.

"Make my own transcriptions," Baron said proudly, pointing to a turntable on the bench. "Quality is as good as they do at NBC. All those are shows I've recorded. Someday maybe I'll be able to make copies and sell them to people. Right now it's not legal."

I wondered why people would want to buy old radio shows when they could listen to new ones for nothing, but I just nodded in understanding.

"Martin. . . ." I prodded.

"Adams, Andrews, maybe Anderson," said Baron. "Wanted to make records, transcriptions of his family. Said he wanted to surprise them, hide the microphone under the dining-room table, play it back for them later. Keep it as a family memory."

"That's what he said?" I asked.

"That's what he said," Baron repeated. "Mind if I use a bad word?"

"No."

"I thought it was a bunch of bullshit."

"Why?"

"Couldn't imagine seeing the guy around the Sunday table with grandma, mom, and the kids passing around the mashed potatoes and fried chicken. You say he's your friend?"

"I met him once or twice," I said.

Baron fiddled with his earphones, plugged the wire into a jack on a phonograph on the bench, pulled it out again and said, "Something funny about him."

"Funny?"

"Fake," he said. "Pretending. Laughing but not seeing anything funny. You know what I mean? You run into people like that sometimes."

"I know what you mean. So he bought equipment to make secret recordings?"

"That's what he said," said Baron. "Bought lots of blank records too."

"He ever mention a George Hall to you?" I asked.

Baron thought and then shook his head.

"Never mentioned anyone to me that I remember. Like I said, he was an odd little guy. Listen, you interested in a phonograph? I'll throw in six transcriptions of Sherlock Holmes shows."

"I thought you said it was illegal to sell radio shows."

"The law is murky," Baron said.

"I think I'll take the brown Bakelite radio," I said.

When he made out the sales slip, Baron said, "Do me a favor. If you talk to your friend Martin, don't mention anything I said about him. He's a good customer."

"I promise I won't mention anything either of us said."

I took my new radio and considered making a stop at the Chinese restaurant. It smelled good. It smelled like a Chinese restaurant. But I had another stop to make.

I put the radio on the floorboard in front of the passenger seat and headed for Wesley Flynn's Typewriter Repair and Maintenance.

There had been no phonograph or radio in Bruno Volkman's apartment. And I hadn't seen a typewriter, although I hadn't done a complete search of the closet where I'd found his body. I had the feeling that Bruno didn't keep his recording equipment or his typewriter in his apartment where someone might find it and have some questions about what they were doing there.

Wesley Flynn's shop was a wooden one-story building that had once been painted gray. It sagged on one side as if it were considering sitting down.

Parking was no problem. There was a small lot next to the building and only one battered small truck in it. The door stuck when I tried to open it, and I had to give it a push with my shoulder.

Baron's had been neatly laid out. Flynn's was a mess. Typewriters sat on shelves, on the floor, on top of each other. Some had white tags on their shift arms. There were machines with most of the keys missing and others without a roller bar.

Behind a counter, next to a cash register, sat an old man wearing a green visor. He sat on a stool reading an old issue of *Life* magazine. The cover of the magazine showed Fred Astaire dancing with his small son.

"Flynn?" I asked.

He looked up and sighed. I had disturbed his reading.

"Yeah."

"Looking for a typewriter," I said.

"Turn your head any direction," the old man said, tilting his head back to get a better look at me from under his visor. "See something you like, I can put it in shape for you. Got a few that work pretty good just as they sit."

"I'm looking for a typewriter a friend of mine may have bought from you," I said, taking Volkman's photograph from my pocket and moving to the counter.

The old man squinted at the photograph.

"Awhile ago," he said. "Maybe six, eight months. Remington. Nice machine. Old. About 1912. Probably should have held on to it till it became an antique. Probably would have if I thought I'd live long enough so's it would be old enough to sell as one."

"He only came in once?" I asked.

"Came in four, five times. Kept messing up the keys, couldn't change a ribbon, didn't know how to clean it. Said he was writing a book about horses. No one asked him, but he told me. Didn't look like the horse type, but who knows?"

"Who knows?" I said.

"So you don't want to buy a typewriter?" he asked. "You just want to find the guy who bought the old Remington?"

"Yes."

"You some kind of process server?"

"Something like that," I said.

"You look like you've seen your share," he said. "I've got an address from him somewhere."

"That might help."

"Cost you," he said. "Five bucks."

"If it's not on Boyle Avenue, I might buy it."

He pulled out three cigar boxes from under the counter and started to go through the first one, taking sales slips and flopping them in front of him.

"Here," he said. "Two-oh-two West First."

"That's the Los Angeles Times building," I said.

He began stuffing the sales slips back in the box, leaving the one he had just fished out on the side.

"What name did he give?"

The old man glanced at the slip again.

"Fred Lowe."

Bruno Volkman had a hell of a lot of names.

"Fred Lowe who lives in the Los Angeles Times building," I

said, pulling out my wallet. I handed him a five-dollar bill, which he put into his cash register.

Bruno Volkman had purchased recording equipment and a typewriter he didn't want traced to him. Somewhere, there were recordings and typed files that Volkman had plans for. Since he had contacted Cary Grant, I figured he had decided to do some selling.

"How's business?" I asked politely, putting my wallet back in my pocket.

The old man looked around.

"Nonexistent," he said. "Don't much care. Got a little house all paid for, enough in the bank, and not that many years to worry about. Place is about to fall down, and I lost interest in fixing these damn machines before the war even started."

"Sorry," I said.

"Just the way things are," he said. "I've got a good offer for this lot. Some movie director's wife wants to build a Hungarian restaurant, or maybe it's Rumanian. I'll take it and throw in all the contents of this building. In fact, that'll be a condition. They take this junk or I don't sell. You want a free typewriter?"

"No, thanks," I said.

He shrugged and went back to his *Life* magazine. I went back to my Crosley. My radio was still there.

When I arrived at the Farraday after stopping for a couple of hot dogs and a Pepsi, Violet waved me over before I could go through the door to Shelly's office.

"He's in the chair," she whispered.

"He?"

"Mountain," she said even more softly. "Dr. Minck needs complete quiet."

"And I need to get to my office, humble though it may be," I said.

"Just another minute or two," she said. "He's been in there for almost an hour."

There was no sound from beyond the door.

"You've got a message," she said, moving to her little desk and retrieving a small slip of paper. I looked at it. "Mr. Leach says to call him."

"Thanks, Violet," I said.

"Nice radio," she said, looking at the Bakelite model I carried under my right arm.

"Thanks," I said. "I didn't want to leave it in the car."

The door to Shelly's office opened, and Sheldon Minck, head covered in perspiration, cigar moist in the corner of his mouth, glasses about to fall to the floor, blood forming crawling blobs on his dirty white lab coat, stood before us with a smile.

"Got it," he said, showing us a tooth that looked very much like the one that was sitting in my pocket. "You can see, right here, the decay. Must have been hurting him like the devil."

In the chair behind him, Mountain groaned as he started to wake up.

Shelly grinned and raised his eyebrows, then turned to his patient. I followed him. Mountain sat up groggily, his eyes trying to focus.

Sheldon Minck held the tooth up for him to see.

"Here it is," he said.

Mountain looked at the tooth and then touched it.

"Mirror," he said.

Sheldon reached for the small round mirror on the tray next to the dental chair. He rubbed the surface of the mirror on a relatively bloodless part of his lab coat and handed it to the big, bearded man, who held it out and examined himself.

"How do I look?" he asked me.

"Fierce," I said.

Actually, he looked ugly as hell. He had looked ugly before losing the teeth. He looked a lot worse now.

"Really?" he asked.

"I wouldn't lie to you," I said.

Mountain managed a facial expression that I'm sure was intended as a grin.

"Good job, Doc," he said taking Sheldon's hand.

"Skill," said Sheldon. "It's what I do, how I help my patients."

I went to my office as Sheldon was almost crushed to the floor as he tried to help Mountain to his feet.

First things first. I called Cary Grant. He answered after two rings.

"Peters," he said. "Did you find anything?"

"No George Hall," I said. "But Volkman was transcribing conversations and probably typing them up."

"Can you find them?" he asked.

"I can try."

"Good, meanwhile I've got some news. Bad news. I checked on Cookinham, got his address from the studio. He has a house in Van Nuys, a modest place."

"You went there?"

"Yes."

"And you found Cookinham? What did he say?"

"Nothing. He was dead. I knocked at the door, but there was no answer. The door was open. I went in and called for him. The place was dark, shades down and a bad smell. I found him in the bedroom with a gun in his hand and a bullet in his head."

"Suicide?"

"Maybe," he said. "I didn't look too carefully, but I did see a typewriter and something that might have been recording equipment on the kitchen table."

"Any records?" I asked.

"I didn't stay around long enough to look. If I get caught in a situation like that, you can kiss my career good-bye."

"I'll have to go take a look," I said. "What's the address?"

He gave it to me.

"Be careful," he said. "Peters, I've never really seen anything like that before."

"I have," I said.

"I kept thinking it was like a movie," said Grant quietly. "Not quite real. A set. B-movie lighting. Makeup. Maybe it's because I really didn't know the man."

"Maybe," I said. "I'll get back to you after I check on the house."

The house was small, a one-bedroom off of Tampa Avenue. The grass in the front yard was recently mowed, and a small bird I couldn't identify was perched on the mailbox at the curb. The Aldrich family could have lived there.

There were hedges between the houses on the street and no house at all across from Cookinham's. Crosleys are easy to remember, so I parked a block away and walked back slowly, whistling "*Hindustan*," ready to give a smile to anyone I might meet. Maybe I'd even say, "Top of the mornin.'"

But I didn't meet anyone. The door to Cookinham's house was open, just as Cary Grant had said. I walked in, closed it behind me, and looked around. There was the smell Grant had warned me about, but there was also lots of sun coming through the windows. Grant had said the shades were down. I decided to hurry.

Neat little living room, not much furniture, but full bookshelves against the walls. There were a few record albums about eye level on a shelf near a window.

I removed one. It was Nelson Eddy singing his favorite arias. There was a photograph of Eddy on the cover, his mouth open in song. I tried all the albums. Strauss waltzes, Rise Stevens singing favorite arias, Bing Crosby Christmas songs, Renata Tebaldi in *Tosca*.

I moved to the bedroom. Cookinham, in his pajamas, was seated on the bed looking at the mirror across from him with dead eyes and mouth open. He looked pretty much the way he did in the photograph in my pocket, but he had acquired a hole in his right temple and a gun in his right hand.

There were three framed photographs on his dresser. One was the same as the photograph in my pocket. The second, a smaller one, was of a younger Cookinham standing in front of a waterfall, and the last was of a trio of girls about twelve years old, arms around each others' shoulders, grinning at the camera. Something about their clothes made me think the picture had not been taken in the United States. The interesting photograph was the one that was missing. There was a very thin layer of dust on the top of the dresser and the faint but definite outline of the edges of a larger frame.

A jacket was draped over a chair near the bed. I checked the pockets. Empty. Then I checked his trousers, which were neatly laid out on the same chair. No notebook. A wallet with thirty-eight dollars. No cards. I made a quick search of drawers and the closet. Nothing very interesting. There was no suicide note.

In the kitchen, a typewriter and a fake-leather covered box about the size of a phonograph player sat on a small Formica table. Inside the box was a turntable with an attached microphone. There was no paper in or near the typewriter and no record on or near the turntable.

I could have done a better job, but I remembered those shades being up and decided to get out fast. As it turned out, I got out just fast enough. I was halfway up the block with my car in sight when a Los Angeles police car sped down the street and came to a screeching halt in front of Cookinham's house.

About forty minutes later and low on gas, I was back at Mrs. Plaut's boardinghouse. Mrs. Plaut did not greet me when I came in. The door to her rooms was closed. I trudged up the stairs with my new radio and the pile of papers I had accumulated.

I put the radio and the papers on the table next to the phone on the second-floor landing, dug out some coins, and called Cary Grant. The phone rang. It kept ringing. Eight times. I was about to hang up, when he came on.

"Yes?"

"It's me, Peters," I said. "I went there. Didn't find much."

"We should tell the police," he said.

"They already know."

I told him about the two FBI agents.

"That's not good," he said. I didn't say anything, so he went on. "The people I'm working with need to find this Hall and whoever else is involved."

"The people you're working with?"

"I can't really say more," he said. "I'm afraid you'll just have to trust me."

"I'm afraid I will," I agreed.

"I've got to run," he said. "I have a meeting in an hour about a new movie. The script looks good. I get to go back to my roots, play a shiftless cockney. They've got Ethel Barrymore lined up to play my mother."

"Good luck," I said.

"I'll be back in two hours," he said. "Call me if you find out anything more."

He hung up and so did I.

Gunther was in his room when I knocked. He told me to come in. He was seated at his desk, two books open in front of him and a pen in his hand.

"Toby," he said. "I'm afraid we still have no luck in our search for George Hall. I've located a bedridden Negro who was a railroad porter, and another George Hall is a chicken rancher, who moved many months ago when his wife died."

"Jeremy went home?"

"Yes," said Gunther. "He said he was going to write a poem

about the search. I am not of a creative bent of mind. I can see no poetry in what we did today."

"I bought a radio," I said, holding it up. "I also found another body."

I placed the stack of papers on the desk next to one of Gunther's open books. On top of the stack was the photograph of Volkman and Cookinham.

"They're both dead," I said.

I told him everything that had happened and what I had learned.

"The way I see it," I went on. "Cookinham and Volkman were making secret recordings of a group of Nazis or Nazi sympathizers. They were probably part of the group. Maybe they wanted the recordings for protection. Maybe they wanted to work some blackmail or sell them to the highest bidder, or maybe they just planned to make a deal with the FBI if the group ever got caught. Somehow they found out Grant was interested in finding Nazi sympathizers. They knew he had money. They made a deal. The bad guys found out, killed them both."

"George Hall," said Gunther.

"Looks that way," I said.

"What can I do?" Gunther asked.

"You can look through that pile of Nazi flyers and stuff I got from Volkman's apartment. Some of it's in German."

"I will do so immediately," he said. "You look tired."

"Guess I am," I said.

My neck and shoulder had settled into a steady tolerable ache.

"I think I'll lie down for a while and listen to my new radio."

And that's just what I did.

The Longines Symphonette was playing something with no melody, which was fine with me. I didn't pull out my mattress, just laid down on the sofa with my head on the "God Bless Us" pillow Mrs. Plaut had made when I had first moved in.

It took me about five minutes to find a position where my head didn't touch anything and my neck and shoulder weren't annoyed. Then I slept. Dreamless, vaguely aware of the music.

I slept till I was awakened by the knock at my door. I opened my eyes and said, "Come in."

Gunther was there. He had something in his hand and he was clearly excited.

"I know where to find George Hall," he said.

CHAPTER 11

"IT IS AN irony worthy of Gogol," Gunther said.

He was sitting in the wooden desk chair in his room.

I was sitting in his firm low-legged armchair.

"Worthy of Gogol," I agreed.

I was holding the three-fold brochure for the School of Performance at Caroll College. Gunther had circled something on the back page under a small photograph of the building where I had talked acting with Jacklyn Wright.

"Andrew George Hall," I read.

"It is a place, not a person," said Gunther.

I had called Cary Grant when Gunther had told me the news no more than five minutes earlier. Grant had never heard of Caroll College. He said he would come to Mrs. Plaut's as soon as he could get there.

And so Gunther and I waited, trying to come up with a plan or two for Grant when he arrived. We couldn't go to the police. All we had was the name of a building on a college campus. And we couldn't walk in and accuse anyone of anything. We had no evidence. What we did have was the information that Jacklyn Wright had told me about Bruno Volkman taking night school acting classes with her under a fake name. She had also told me she didn't know who George Hall was when we were standing inside George Hall.

"I've got an idea," I said, standing up and plunging my hands into my pockets in search of change. I found Mountain's tooth and some nickels, dimes, and quarters. I asked Gunther if he had more. He removed a stack of change from the center drawer of his desk and handed it to me. "Be right back."

With the brochure in my hand, I used the boardinghouse pay phone to call the number neatly printed on the back.

"School of Performance Arts," came the voice I thought belonged to the woman I had met in the school office.

"Good afternoon," I said, trying for a refined tone. "My name is Spaulding. I have one of your brochures about your acting program. I would be very much interested."

"Full-time, part-time, or evening school?" she asked.

"Evening," I said. "I work days."

"You have any acting experience?" she asked.

"A little. Community theater in Portland. I played the mayor in *Our Town*. The local paper said I was adequate. I knew my lines, which was more than could be said for some of the others in our company. I have a passion for the stage."

"Tuesday nights at seven," she said. "Stop in the office with a check for twenty dollars. You have the brochure, so you know this is a six-week course. The course started last week, but Professor Wright can give you and other late enrollees an extra session at the end."

"Fine. Fine," I said. "Is that the only evening acting class you have?"

"We have an ongoing class for advanced students," she said.

"Can I try that? I do have experience."

"That's a closed class. Only regulars till the session ends."

"And when does it end?"

"It doesn't," she said. "It continues."

"Are there many people in that class?"

"Nine," she said, "but you really can't. . . ."

"I understand," I said. "I understand. I'm just excited by the thought of doing more acting."

"Your name?" she asked flatly.

What name had I given her? Right.

"Spaulding, Melvin Spaulding."

"Be here just before seven, Mr. Spaulding. Check or cash for twenty dollars."

She hung up. So did I. I went back and reported to Gunther. We were considering more options when the doorbell rang downstairs.

"I'll go," I said.

I was getting used to the throb in my neck and shoulder, and my scalp, where the stitches were, had begun to itch.

Mrs. Plaut beat me to the door. I was halfway down the steps. She was standing in the open doorway, looking at Cary Grant in light gray slacks, a tieless white shirt, and a perfectly pressed charcoal sports jacket with a white handkerchief peeking out of the pocket.

"Good afternoon," he said with a smile, glancing up at me.

"Relatively," Mrs. Plaut said. "I opened a jar of pickled avocados just minutes ago, but they were spoiled."

"Sorry to hear that," Grant said, looking to me for help as I hurried down the stairs.

"I have one room left," she said. "That's why the sign is in the window. Room and Board."

"He's not looking for a room, Mrs. Plaut," I said, getting to the bottom of the steps. "He's here to see me."

Mrs. Plaut gave me a slight glance and looked back at Grant, who smiled.

"I know you," she said. "You're in the newspapers sometimes."

"I'm afraid so," Grant conceded.

"You're the fire commissioner," she said.

"Right," I jumped in.

"Why is the fire commissioner here to see you?" Mrs. Plaut asked me.

"I've volunteered to help organize the firemen's ball," I said.

"Is that true?" she asked Grant.

"The fire department is grateful for all the help it can get," said Grant. "Suppose the Japanese sent a fleet and started firing cannons at the city."

Mrs. Plaut shook her head.

"The Japanese are running," she said. "They're not the ones to worry about. You see a Japanese and you know he's Japanese unless he's Chinese or something else from over there. You see a Japanese and you're on the ready. No, the ones to worry about are the Huns. They look like us only smarmy. They could sabotage."

"They could," Grant agreed, once again looking at me for help.

"We've got to do some planning now, Mrs. Plaut," I said.

"Where?"

"In Gunther's room," I said, heading for the stairs with Grant behind me. He was looking back at Mrs. Plaut.

"Pleasure to meet you," he said. "May I say you remind me of my mother?"

"You may say it if the reminder is a positive one," she said.

"It is," said Grant.

At the top of the stairs, Grant said, "She does remind me of my mother back in England. She's a little . . ."

"Unfocused," I supplied as we moved to Gunther's door.

"Yes," said Grant. "Unfocused."

Gunther got out of his chair to shake Grant's hand and offered his guest the armchair where I had been sitting. Grant sat and I moved to the small sofa against the wall in front of the ceiling-high bookcase.

I handed Grant the brochure and told him about George Hall and my call to Caroll College.

"Volkman was in that advanced class?" Grant asked.

"Jacklyn Wright told me he was," I said.

Grant sat thinking for a while, rubbing the fingers of his right hand across his lips.

"Try this," he said, sitting forward. "A Nazi cell. They meet every week as an advanced acting class. Doors closed. They pay their tuition, make their plans, maybe turn in whatever it is they know and get their orders."

"Maybe," I said.

"Volkman said George Hall," Grant said. "His dying words."

"It is possible," said Gunther.

"Sure it is," said Grant. "Volkman knew what room they met in every week. He and Cookinham set up equipment to record their meetings. Blackmail, protection."

"Why come to you?" I asked.

"Maybe they got the idea that someone was suspicious," Grant said, standing up and pacing now as he thought. "They knew I'd pay for the names of the people in the group. They wanted to get out fast, maybe take their transcriptions with them, try to blackmail the group or maybe try to sell them to me."

"Why would they think you would be interested in purchasing such material?" Gunther asked.

"I'm an American," Grant said. "I became a citizen a little over a year ago, but I still have my roots in England. From time to time I pass information onto British Intelligence, information I get from other Brits in the industry who keep their eyes and ears open."

"You're a spy?" asked Gunther.

"Let's say I'm involved in helping the Allied cause in any way I can," Grant said. "I tried to enlist in the American army. They said I'd be more help doing U.S.O. shows and visiting veterans' hospitals. So that's what I do, but it's not enough."

"I understand," said Gunther.

"So," I said. "What do we do? I've got two FBI agents wondering what I'm doing. I could talk to them."

"You might try it," Grant said with no great enthusiasm. "I say we get more information, a list of names of people in that so-called acting class, something the FBI or my contacts can check on."

"And how do we do that?" Gunther asked.

I knew the answer, but I let Grant say it.

"What name did you give the woman over the phone?"

"Melvin Spaulding," I said.

"Right," Grant said, halting his pacing. "Melvin Spaulding has to show up for that advanced acting class tonight."

"I can't," I said. "Jacklyn Wright knows me. And you can't. Everybody knows you."

"I could do it," said Gunther. "I have acted, been on the stage."

"Gunther was in *The Wizard of Oz*," I said.

"You were? What were you?"

"A Munchkin soldier and a flying monkey," Gunther said, straightening his vest. "It was not a pleasant experience."

"I don't like it," Grant said. "Maybe I can get someone through my contacts."

"We have but a few hours," Gunther said, looking at his pocket watch. "I'm perfectly capable of taking care of myself, and with my knowledge of German I might discover something of value. There is one advantage in being a little person. People look at you, but they do not fear you. I do not blend in with the crowd, but I am often ignored at its center."

Grant and I looked at each other. We both nodded.

"Good," said Gunther. "I will go, and attempt to enter the group and find a way to get a list of names."

"Better idea," I said. "I'll wait till you're in the class and get into the office, try to find a list."

"I'm going with you," said Grant.

"You think that's a good idea?"

"The truth? I don't know," said Grant. "I do know I want to be there."

The door to Gunther's room sprang open.

Mrs. Plaut stood there with a tray. On the tray was a teapot, cups, and a platter of neatly cut-in-half sandwiches. She moved to Gunther's desk, placed the tray on it, and turned to Grant, who stood next to her.

"You are not the fire commissioner," she said.

"I'm sorry," he said.

"You are Warren Harding's son," she said. "I recognize you now."

"I'm working with the fire commissioner," Grant said.

"What?"

"I'm working with the fire commissioner," he said louder.

"I like you," she said, touching his arm, "but you are not much of an actor. You are fibbing. Why you are fibbing, I do not know. Perhaps in time you will all see fit to take me into your confidence. I descend from a loyal American family, as Mr. Peelers can attest."

"Very loyal," I said. I could have added that they were also eccentric, violent, confused, and constituted a historical threat to the nation.

"All right," said Grant with a sigh. "I'm Cary Grant, the movie actor. We've stumbled on a nest of spies. They've already killed two men. We plan to stop them."

"The three of you?" she asked.

"The three of us," Grant said.

"That is a silly story, which insults my intelligence," she said. "I have made you dark tea and cucumber-and-butter sandwiches and you tell me stories. I wash my hands of this trio, I can tell you. Personally, I think you're planning to rob a bank."

She closed the door behind her.

"I like that woman," said Grant. "I'm not always sure what she's talking about, but there's something likable about her."

"We know," I said, "but when you live under her roof, she can make you very tired very fast."

We had three cars. We decided to take two, mine and Grant's. When the evening was over, Grant could go home and so could Gunther and I.

Before we left, Gunther said he had to make a phone call.

"It should take me no more than a minute," he said.

Grant and I ate cucumber-and-butter sandwiches and drank dark tea until Gunther returned and said he was ready.

Mrs. Plaut was waiting at the bottom of the stairs, hands on hips, glaring at Grant.

"Where have I seen you?" she demanded.

In response, Grant moved into the alcove next to her and did a quick back flip.

"The circus," she said.

Grant grinned and wiped his hands.

Mrs. Plaut went back into her rooms with a look of satisfaction on her face. In front of her Pistolero screeched wildly.

Grant drove but I was giving directions since I knew the way to Caroll College. After I'd removed my flashlight and gun from the Crosley, Gunther had hopped in, ready to follow us. The Crosley seemed to have been designed for people his size.

We listened to the news as we drove. The Germans were on the run. As many as three thousand American bombers were tearing up Northern Germany. And on the other side of the world, Liberator bombers had unloaded ten tons of bombs on Japanese bases in Lampong, Thailand.

"We can still call in the FBI," I said.

"They won't believe us," Grant said. "And even if they did, it would take them days, weeks to do anything about it. If I can get the names Volkman had for me, I can get them to people who will be more than willing to step a little outside the law. I don't know how much time we have. Peters, these people are planning sabotage."

"Can I ask you a question?"

"Certainly," Grant said.

"Strictly confidential," I said. "How did you get into this."

"I started with a fellow from British Intelligence who asked me to keep my ears open for people in the movie industry making anti-Jewish remarks, possible Nazi spies trying to find people who were sympathizers."

"And?"

"I found more of them in my wife's social circle than in the industry," he said. "Barbara didn't seem to notice. One turned out to be a person I thought was a friend. He's under surveillance now. Then, British Intelligence asked me to do a few more things here and there. I was more than willing."

The Caroll College parking lot wasn't full at seven at night. There were a few lights on in offices or classrooms in the building next to the parking lot.

Gunther pulled in alongside of us and stepped out.

"A request, Toby," he said. "And I hope you take no offense from it."

"What?"

"Permit me to clean the interior of your automobile," he said.

"Permission granted," I said and led the way to the concrete path next to the building in front of us. Some of the buildings on campus were completely dark. The School of Performance wasn't brightly lit, but a light shone from inside the double doors.

A few people were coming up behind us from the parking lot.

"Gunther, you go in. We'll be behind you. Stall as long as you can while we try to find the class list."

Gunther nodded in understanding and walked with dignity toward the double door. Grant and I moved to the dark side of the building.

From the shadows, we watched a trio of men moving toward the building. They were talking quietly. We couldn't make out what they were saying.

"Time?" I asked.

Grant held up his wrist to catch some dim light.

"A few minutes after seven," he said. "Class should be starting."

"Let's go," I said, moving back in the darkness toward the dim outline of a window.

If I had figured this right, the window was to the office behind the reception area where I had gotten directions to Jacklyn Wright's class.

The window was about chest high and locked. The room inside was dark. With my pocket knife I had no trouble popping the latch and opening the window. I clambered in and Grant nimbly jumped in behind me. I closed the window and pulled down the shade before turning on my flashlight.

We were standing in a small neat office. Polished dark wood desk with nothing on top of it. Matching chair. A trio of simple wooden chairs with arms. A bookcase on one wall running from floor to ceiling. A pair of file cabinets on the other wall and framed Audubon prints of water birds.

I went to the desk drawer, pulled it open, and found a small box of calling cards that told me we were in the office of Lawrence Toddhunter, Dean of the School of Performance. There were no photographs on the dean's desk.

We checked the file cabinets and the desk for class lists but didn't find any, so we moved to the door. I unlocked it, and we stepped into the reception area. There was light coming from the corridor outside the room, but not much. "Flashlight off," I whispered.

Then, "Over there," to Grant to let him know where I'd had seen file cabinets when I had last been in this room.

We went to the cabinets, where I clicked my flashlight back on and we began to look for the class list. The problem wasn't a lack of lists. There were hundreds of them. In the third drawer down, we found the class list for the night school's advanced performance class.

"Recognize any of the names?" I whispered.

"No," said Grant. "But if we are talking about a group of spies, they probably wouldn't use their own names. I've got to take a longer look at them."

We moved to the door to the corridor. I unlocked it and opened it slowly. There was no one out there. We turned in the direction of the theater I had been in and stopped.

Voices were coming from inside the room. People were talking quickly, and the distinctive voice of Gunther Wherthman was responding. They were speaking German. I looked at Grant, who shrugged to let me know he couldn't understand, either.

He motioned for me to follow him, and we walked farther down the corridor to a room labeled "Backstage and Storeroom." We went in. It was dark, and we needed the flashlight as we moved down the long narrow passage, made more narrow by boards and backdrops and assorted props leaning against the wall.

On the other side of the thin wall, we could hear the sound of German. At the end of the passage were three stairs going up. We tiptoed up and found another door on our left. The sound of voices was louder now.

I opened the door, and through the crack we could see the small stage on which Gunther stood looking out at six men and three women, one of whom was Jacklyn Wright. All were casually dressed. Four of the men were wearing shirts chosen to show their muscles.

"I said to speak English," Jacklyn Wright said. "If someone should hear. . . ."

"Very well," said Gunther. "I will say it once more."

"You will say it as many times as we wish it said," said one of the bodybuilders.

"I have been sent by Reichfuhrer Grembauer to warn you that your security has been compromised. One among you is a traitor," said Gunther.

This was not the scenario we had worked on. Gunther was improvising, and it looked as if his audience wasn't buying his act.

"Why not use the usual channels?" asked another man.

"Because," Gunther answered. "He is not certain of the loyalty of his messengers."

"But he trusts you?" another bodybuilder asked with a smirk.

"Implicitly," said Gunther.

"There are no midgets in the Third Reich," the man challenged.

"I am not a midget," Gunther said. "I am a dwarf and I am also special envoy. If I were not, how could I know you were here? If I were not, why would I come alone and not simply go to the FBI or the police?"

"Call him," demanded one of the women.

"It will take him at least half an hour to get here," Jacklyn Wright said.

"Good," said Gunther. "Call him, tell him to come here. We will wait. Meanwhile, I suggest that no one leave this room alone. Anyone could be the traitor."

I closed the door and whispered to Grant.

"You recognize any of them?"

"Three of them, two of the men and one woman," he said. "I don't know their names, but one's a secretary at RKO and the others are actors. What now?"

"We call the FBI and get them over here fast," I said, "but we tell them to wait till whoever those people in there are going to call gets here."

"Sounds like a good plan," said Grant.

We went back down the passageway. When I tried the door, it wouldn't open.

"Locked from the outside," I said.

"We can break it down," Grant said.

"Too much noise. They'd be all over us."

"Then?"

"Only one way to go."

We went back down the passage to the stage door.

When I opened it again, one of the women and two of the men were coming in the doors to the theater. They were in a hurry.

"We reached him," one of the men said. "He knows no Reichfuhrer Grembauer. This is some kind of trick or trap. We are to eliminate him and disperse immediately."

"Stop," Gunther said with confidence. "It is clear. He is the traitor."

"Who?" asked Jacklyn Wright.

"The very person you just called," Gunther said.

"And what is that person's name?" an older man with rimless spectacles asked.

He had Gunther with that one.

"I know only his true name, not his false identity," said Gunther.

"Kill him," said the man with glasses.

"I'm going to distract them," Grant said. "Try to sneak around them to get some help."

I started to protest, but Grant was already past me and onto the stage standing next to Gunther.

"All right," Grant announced with confidence. "You're all under arrest."

With my back to the wall, I edged out into the shadows and started down toward the left wall of the small theater. The nine people looking at the stage all recognized Grant. They stood in stunned silence for a few seconds. I kept inching along the wall.

"Just line up in the aisle," Grant said, motioning toward the aisle. "Women first and then men by height, smallest in the front."

I was halfway to the back of the theater when Jacklyn Wright said, "Get them."

One of the men started toward the stage. The other men and women seemed confused by what was happening. One of the women spotted me, pointed and shouted, "They're here."

The group was within feet of the auditorium exit when the doors suddenly opened inward. Blocking the doorway were Jeremy Butler and Mountain. The group panicked. Four of the men made the mistake of running at Jeremy and Mountain. All four were on the floor seconds later.

The bodybuilder who had been rushing toward Grant and Gunther suddenly changed his mind and headed for the door to the passageway Grant and I had come through. Grant got to him before the man could open the door.

The man turned, throwing a wide right at Grant's head. Grant ducked well below the swing and jabbed a fast left into the man's stomach. The man went down.

"What are you doing?" Jacklyn Wright said, facing me. "We were trying to hold our regular acting class and you and your friends have trespassed and beaten us. I'm calling the police."

"Let's go together," I said.

I left with Jeremy and Mountain herding the group into the first two rows of the auditorium.

"I'm coming with you," Grant said, jumping from the stage and following us. "I've got a call to make too."

"You are Cary Grant, aren't you?" Jacklyn said.

Grant nodded.

"What are you doing here?" she asked. "The college lawyers will make you pay for this."

"We'll see," said Grant.

We went into the office Grant and I had recently been in, and I ushered Jacklyn toward the phone. Grant headed for the dean's office in search, I assumed, of another phone.

Jacklyn reached for the phone.

"Sure you want the police?" I asked.

She put the phone to her ear.

"Suit yourself," I said with a shrug. "They're going to want to know who everyone in your class is, their real names, backgrounds."

"What do you want?" she asked.

"The real names and the name of your leader," I said.

"What leader?"

"The one your friend called for instructions," I said.

"No," she said. "I'll take my chances with the police. It will ruin your friend Cary Grant's career, breaking into an acting class, assaulting a student. And you, what will you and your friends say? You, too, broke in on an acting class. You have no evidence of anything. Well?"

"No," I said. "I can't let a pack of Nazis loose. And when we all accuse you of being a German spy, the newspapers and the college administration will be all over you."

"Stalemate?" she asked, hands on hips.

"No," I said.

Grant came back into the room.

"All taken care of," he said, rubbing his hands together and smiling.

"The lady says your career will be ruined if the police come in," I said.

"We'll just have to wait and see, won't we?" he said with confidence.

I called the police, and we escorted Jacklyn back to the auditorium, where she sat on one of the aisle seats in the third row. Jeremy and Mountain stood guard, while Gunther sat in the last row by himself. I joined him.

"That wasn't the plan," I said.

"I took it upon myself to call Jeremy from Mrs. Plaut's," Gunther said. "I thought it might be prudent."

"That's not what I mean," I said. "*That* was a good idea. But the Nazi act. . . ."

"They were not going to let me in," he said. "I even threatened to sue them for keeping a qualified citizen from attending a public class for which he was well qualified."

"And? . . . "

"It came to me," he said. "I started to speak to them in German, hoping I could convince them or at least keep their attention till you accomplished your mission or arrived."

"You succeeded," I said.

Six policemen in uniform and two in plain clothes were there within ten minutes, guns drawn, striding down the aisle.

Grant leaned back against the stage with his arms folded. The older of the two uniformed cops looked at him and nodded toward the entrance to the theater. On his way past me toward the door, Grant whispered, "Sorry. I'll give you a call tomorrow."

I watched him leave and turned back to the cops.

"We'll start with . . ." the older plainclothes cop said.

"Me," said Jacklyn Wright. "These men broke in, disrupted my class, and beat my students."

"Why?" asked the cop.

She hadn't considered this question.

"I assume they are drunk," she said.

The younger plainclothesman smelled my breath, Gunther's, Jeremy's, and Mountain's.

"Seem sober to me," he said.

"They did disrupt my class," she insisted.

"Why?" The question from the older cop was aimed at me.

"They're all Nazis," I said. "They're using this class to cover their meetings. You check their backgrounds and. . . ."

"They're all Nazis?" the older cop repeated. "How do you know?"

I stopped myself before mentioning the murders of Volkman and Cookinham. I didn't want that door opened.

"Check on them," I repeated.

"And why did you let Cary Grant go?" Jacklyn demanded.

"Cary Grant?" asked the older cop, looking at the younger one. "Cary Grant was in here?"

"You know he was," she shouted.

"Just saw a janitor," the cop said. "I'd have recognized Cary Grant. You, Mel?"

"I'd have recognized him," said the younger cop.

"Any of you?" the older cop asked the uniforms.

They all shook their heads "no." They knew when they were being led to water.

"I think we'll just take the whole class over to the station and give the FBI a call," the older cop said. "Not that I think they'll find anything, but these are dangerous times and I've got a son who lost an arm in France last year. You'll have to humor me."

"I . . . we want a lawyer," she said, glaring at me.

"We'll talk to our captain about that at the station," the cop said. Then he looked at me and added, "The two big ones? They with you?"

"Yes," I said.

"And the little one?"

"Yes."

"You've got one strange army," he said, turning to the uniformed cops and adding, "Anderson, call for a paddy wagon."

One of the uniformed cops put his gun away and headed for the door.

This was all going too easily. I decided not to wait until the cop decided what to do with us.

"If you don't need me and my friends anymore . . . " I began.

"You're coming with us too," he said. "We've got lots of room, lots of coffee for all of you and your lawyers, plus the FBI. We'll have a party."

One of the bodybuilders suddenly leaped from the first row to the stage and headed for the door to the passageway. Within four feet of the door, Gunther had clambered onto the stage and rammed his head between the man's legs. The big man crumpled with a groan. Gunther smoothed his hair and adjusted his suit.

Less than twenty minutes later we were all seated in a large room in the Burbank police station. I was familiar with the room. I was also familiar with the way cops usually handled roundups like this one. I kept my mouth shut other than to say that we didn't need a lawyer, not yet.

One by one, Jacklyn and her class were taken into a small interrogation room. No one stayed in there more than five minutes. When it was my turn, I went through the door and closed it behind me. The older cop and his partner sat behind a table. There was a chair across from them. The young one named Mel gestured toward it and I sat.

"My name's Alvarez," the older cop said. "Remember me?"

I looked at him again and then remembered. I hadn't seen him in ten years. We had served at the same time when I was a Burbank cop. He looked thirty years older. My recollection was that he was about my age.

"Dennis," I said.

He nodded.

"I'd like to know what's going on," he said.

I opened my mouth and held up a hand.

"I'd like to know, but I've been told not to ask," he said. "I think you screwed up an FBI operation."

It was a distinct possibility.

"Something wrong with your neck?" Alvarez asked.

"Accident," I said.

"If I remember right, you have lots of accidents," he said.

"You remember right."

"You ever balance it out?" he said. "How much you think you average taking in cash in for each accident?"

"I try not to think of it that way," I said.

Alvarez shook his head and looked at Mel.

"Chief of police got a call," said Alvarez. "He called my captain. My captain called me and told us what to do. We're doing it. When we're done doing it, we're letting everyone go. We've got their fingerprints. I've been ordered to turn them over to the FBI, which I will do. I've also been ordered to apologize. That I will not do."

"What about Cary Grant?" I asked.

"We were specifically told that we were not going to find Cary Grant at Caroll College," said Alvarez. "If we saw someone who looked amazingly like him, we were to let him walk. We saw someone."

"We don't like this, Peters," Mel said.

"The FBI wants to talk to you," Dennis said. "They said they'd be coming to see you."

It was my turn to nod.

"Are those people really Nazis?" Dennis asked.

"Yeah, I'm sure," I said.

"Nail the bastards to the wall with railroad spikes," he said.

CHAPTER 12

ON THE DRIVE back to Los Angeles in the Crosley, Gunther asked, "Are you displeased with my behavior?"

"No," I said. "You, Grant, and I would probably be wallpaper if you hadn't called Jeremy."

"I mean about my pretending to be a Nazi envoy," he said with dignity, looking straight forward, barely able to see over the dashboard.

"It was creative," I said. "And it bought us some time. I'm not mad. I asked you to help. You took a chance. I appreciate it."

"I am relieved," Gunther said.

Gunther asked me if he could listen to *Great Moments in Music* on the radio.

"They are doing selections from Puccini's *La Boheme* with Jean Tennyson and Jan Pierce."

"Sounds like fun," I said.

I would have preferred *Mayor of the Town* with Lionel Barrymore and Agnes Moorehead or the Jack Carson show, but overruling Gunther might seem like I was trying to punish him. So we listened, or rather, Gunther listened and I kept driving.

"Listen," Gunther said at one point.

I looked at him. His eyes were closed.

"She is dying," he said. "Mimi. He doesn't know. Plaintive, haunting."

"Yeah," I said.

It was around eleven p.m. by the time we got back to Mrs. Plaut's. I was tired. I wanted to get to a hot shower and let the water hit my shoulder and head for ten minutes while I stood with my eyes closed and tried not to think. That's what I wanted but not what I got.

Mrs. Plaut was standing on the porch as we walked up, her arms folded across her chest.

"There are two men waiting for you in the parlor, Mr. Peelers," she said sternly. "I asked them to return in the A.M. They said it was urgent. I asked them who they were and they told me they were with the Federal Bureau of Fumigation. I informed them that we had no bugs, but perhaps they wish your services in your capacity as an exterminator. Either which way, I cannot see why they couldn't wait till the morning. And with that I say good night and ask you to lock the door behind you."

She turned and went back into the house, leaving the front door open. Gunther and I went in and I closed the door.

"Shall I accompany you?" Gunther asked.

"No, thanks," I said. "This won't take long. I'll talk to you in the morning. Thanks Gunther."

We shook hands, and he gave me that almost nonexistent smile that showed he was reasonably content. As he moved up the stairs, I went into the parlor where Mrs. Plaut had thrown her New Year's Party.

The two FBI men who had stopped me at Carroll College were

sitting on chairs a few feet from each other with their hats on their laps. They were looking up at me.

"Want some coffee?" I asked.

"No, thanks," said the shorter one, Louis D'Argentero.

"No," said the other, taller agent.

I considered sitting, but decided I might get this over with faster if I stood.

"You messed up, Peters," said D'Argentero.

"I didn't get your name," I said to the shorter one.

"Cantwell," said the slightly shorter one.

I nodded.

"You messed up," Cantwell said repeating his partner's words.

I didn't answer.

"We've been watching that cell for months," said Cantwell. "They had no idea. We were trying to get someone inside the organization. We wanted to find out who was heading it."

"Then I messed up," I said.

"You did," said D'Argentero.

"Two men who were members of that cell have been murdered in the last two days, Volkman and Cookinham," Cantwell went on without emotion. "You were found with Volkman's body, and someone said a beat-up Crosley was parked a block from Cookinham's house just before the police got a tip that he was dead."

"Your Crosley," D'Argentero said.

"Is that a question?" I asked.

"No," said Cantwell. "You asked for two days. You have anything?"

"Like? . . . "

"Any lead on whoever runs that Nazi cell," said D'Argentero.

"Or why Volkman and Cookinham were murdered," said Cantwell.

They clearly expected me to say "no." I decided to surprise

them, wake them from their single-tone interrogation, which had me falling asleep on my feet.

"I think Volkman and Cookinham were blackmailing whoever heads the cell," I said. "They had some kind of proof."

"What kind of proof? Proof about what?" Cantwell asked, leaning forward.

"Not sure," I said.

I decided not to mention the recordings for two reasons. First, I wasn't sure. Second, I wanted to hold back something I could work on. I was being paid by Cary Grant. I wanted to give him his money's worth if I could.

"Minding your own business from now on would be a very good idea," Cantwell said, standing up. D'Argentero did the same.

"The police told me James Cagney wasn't at Caroll College tonight," I said.

The two agents looked at me without expression.

"And," I went on, "neither was Joan Crawford, Alice Faye, Paul Muni, or Cary Grant."

"Get some sleep, Peters," Cantwell said, putting on his hat. "You look like a dead horse."

"So none of them was there?" I asked, ignoring the compliment as the two walked past me.

"None of them," said D'Argentero. "Neither was Jimmy Foxx."

"Jimmy Foxx?"

"You a baseball fan?" D'Argentero asked.

"Average," I said.

"Jimmy Foxx quit baseball in 1942," D'Argentero said. "He's thirty-six now, a salesman for a leather goods company. Draft board just called him up. He wasn't in that roundup tonight."

"He's serving his country," Cantwell said. "So are the other people you mentioned."

I got the hint and shut up. The two of them left, and I locked the door behind them as Mrs. Plaut had asked. Her door opened and she stood there, now in a pink robe with a broad pink sash that tried not to slip down past her nonexistent hips.

"What was so much in need of fumigation that they had to come at this hour?" she asked. "They frightened Stillwell."

"Stillwell?"

"That is the new name of my bird," she said. "He likes variety. Pistolero did not suit him. It carried suggestions of Mexican bandits of doubtful character. What about those two fumigators?"

"They're after a very dangerous nest of Nazi weevils."

"Never heard of any such," she said eyeing me suspiciously.

"Very dangerous, hard to root out," I said. "Come from Germany."

"Are they in California?" she asked.

"Some," I said. "Like Japanese beetles."

"My aunt Rose's husband, Lucas, had a brother with an infestation of some small ugly bugs, thousands of them."

"Fascinating," I said.

"Lucas worked in the Armour Packinghouse in Chicago, the stockyards. He knocked cows and sheep senseless with a sledge hammer and someone else cut their throats."

"Even more fascinating," I said.

"It was his brother's house not far from the stockyards that had the bugs," she said.

"How did they get rid of them?" I asked.

"I told you," she said with exasperation. "Lucas hit them with a sledge hammer."

"I mean his brother's bugs."

"Oh, they had to burn the house down. There was no help for it. You may have to burn down the house where these Hun bugs are."

"I may at that," I said. "Now, I've got to get some sleep."

"Breakfast at eight," she said, turning back toward the open door of her room.

I had made it up three stairs when she called behind me, "I am thinking very seriously of getting a dog."

"That's nice," I said.

"A fat, slow, ugly dog that looks like Winston Churchill. One I won't have to chase. One with a placid disposition."

"Sounds great," I said.

"Oh, I nearly forgot," she said. "The man from the circus called, Mr. Leash."

"Leach," I said.

"They are one and the same," she explained. "He said you should call him in the A.M."

"I'll do that," I said.

She went through her door and closed it behind her. I went up the stairs. In my room, I took off my clothes carefully while Dash, who resembled a curled orange pillow, watched. I wanted my clothes in reasonable condition so I could wear them in the morning.

When I was completely undressed, I took more Doc Parry pills and aspirin and wrapped a big towel around my waist. The towel, one of dozens Mrs. Plaut had stockpiled, was white with the words "Dirty Mike's Rooms & Bar" in large red letters across it.

Before I headed for the shower, I pulled out my mattress and laid it on the floor. Then I poured some milk into a bowl for Dash and some Kellogg's Pep into a bowl for me. Dash watched but didn't move.

When I got back from my shower, Dash was on the mattress near my pillow, curled in the same ball he had turned himself into on the sofa.

My Beech-Nut Gum clock said it was almost midnight. I draped the "Dirty Mike" towel over one of the wooden chairs by the table near the window, put on a fresh pair of white boxer shorts, ate a handful of Kellogg's Pep, turned out the light, and got in bed.

If I had dreams, I don't remember them.

We had Trout Plaut for breakfast. It consisted of two filleted slices of brook trout fried in garlic and butter and more than a hint of vanilla. The fish was covered with a thin layer of peanut butter.

"You can't get enough peanut butter," Mrs. Plaut announced as we dug in.

I thought it tasted pretty good, but I saw less than enthusiasm from Emma Simcox, who took a few bites and tried to spread the rest around like a kid hoping to hide her hated vegetables. Ben Bidwell was a salesman of some talent and tact. He shook his head and said with a smile, "Exceptional."

"And nutritious. Peanut butter improves everything," Mrs. Plaut said, eating her trout.

"I don't see any peanut butter on your fish," I said.

"I cannot abide the taste of peanut butter," she said. "That detracts nothing from its value. It speaks only to my experiences as a child, about which I have written in my family history and of which you are well aware, Mr. Peelers."

I didn't remember anything in her family history about peanut butter. She had either never written it and thought she had, or I had simply forgotten or jumped over it. Both and much more were distinct possibilities.

"Got to get going," Bidwell said, standing and wiping his mouth.

"You haven't finished," Mrs. Plaut said.

"Indigestion," Bidwell said, putting his one hand on his chest.

"I'll save the rest for you for tonight," Mrs. Plaut said.

"You are very thoughtful," Bidwell said and made his escape.

I ate all of my fish and so did Gunther. Emma Simcox sat trying to calculate how much she could leave on her plate without drawing the sharp eyes of her aunt.

"Mr. Peelers," Mrs. Plaut said. "Please stop at Ralph's and pick up the items on this list."

She handed me a sheet of paper, along with three one-dollar bills. I looked at the list.

Sirloin steak—two pounds at 49 cents a pound
One pound of oleo—29 cents
One 24-ounce jar of peanut butter—29 cents
Four pounds of potatoes—25 cents
Mott's apple jelly — 12 ounce jar—13 cents

I put the three dollars and the list carefully into the pocket of my jacket.

"Going after those Hun bugs?" Mrs. Plaut asked as I rose.

"Got to stop them before they take over the world," I said.

"Bugs are part of God's great circle of life," she said, looking up at me. "But I hate the filthy little things. That's what bug juice was invented for."

"Amen," I said and left, Gunther at my side.

"What would you have me do today?" Gunther asked.

I wanted to say "nothing" but I was afraid I'd hurt his feelings. I said, instead, "How about doing research on Caroll College, make phone calls, talk to friends, see what you come up with, particularly about the School of Performance."

Gunther nodded.

"I shall do what I can," he said.

Fifteen minutes later, I had my car parked at No-Neck Arnie's. He was too busy with a big dark Buick to talk, so I walked to the Farraday and up the stairs, which was easier on my neck and shoulder than the jolts when the elevator came to each floor.

Jeremy was on the third floor with his mop.

"Thanks for last night," I said.

"You are welcome," he said. "We are having a wake tomorrow night if you can come. Eight o'clock."

"Who died?"

"Ida M. Tarbell," he said. "In Easton, Connecticut. She was eighty-six."

"Ida M. Tarbell?"

"The *Story of Standard Oil.* She was the first to write a book attacking the business practices of a large corporation. She was an inspiration. I'm going to write a poem in her honor. I've asked others to do the same. We'll read them at the wake. Alice and I may publish them in a small folio."

"Put me down for one," I said starting up to the sixth floor.

"You'll write a poem about Ida Tarbell?"

"No, I'll buy a copy of the book," I said, resuming my trudge upward.

"Come if you can," he said.

"I will," I lied.

When I opened the door to the offices of Minck and Peters, Violet greeted me from behind her tiny desk.

"Eddie Booker beat Paul Hartnek on a TKO in the sixth."

I took a five-dollar bill out of my wallet and handed it to her.

"No more bets," I said. "Ever."

She tucked the five into the pocket of her dress with a slightly hurt look.

"Anything else?"

"Jeanne Crain, the actress, 1942 'Camera Girl,' was bitten five times by a wirehaired terrier."

"Sorry to hear that," I said.

"She'll be all right," Violet said with concern. "But her dog, another terrier, was also bitten trying to help her."

I didn't know what to say to that so I reached for the inner door to Sheldon's office.

"He's waiting for you," she said.

"Shelly?"

"No, the good-looking guy who looks like Cary Grant. Is he Grant's double or stand-in or stuntman or something?"

"Something," I said.

"Can he get me an autographed picture?" she asked.

"For Rocky?"

"For me," she said.

"I'll ask."

I went in and found myself facing Shelly. There was no one in the chair.

"I heard you come in," he said, removing the cigar from his mouth.

There were ash stains on his dingy once-white smock, and his office was beginning to show the first small signs of returning to chaos.

"Right," I said, taking a few steps toward my door.

"Why are you angry with me?" he asked, looking genuinely hurt.

"I'm not."

"Jeremy told me about last night. You were there. He was there. Gunther was there, even my favorite patient, Mountain, was there. I could have helped, Toby."

"I'm sure you could have," I said. "I'm sorry. It won't happen again."

"You know I can be very useful," he said.

"I know."

"And you're sorry you didn't call me?"

"Very."

"You know I don't have all that much to do outside of my work here," he said, looking around the room. "Not since Mildred. . . ."

"I'm sorry. I'll call you next time."

"As it happens," he said. "I was busy last night. Mountain has agreed to appear in ads for me with a signed testimonial. I'll get wrestlers, wrestling fans, all kinds of patients. I was working on the ad."

"Sounds good."

"Want to know the motto I plan to put in the ad?"

"Can't wait."

Shelly spread his hands flat in front of him and slowly swept them out as if he were putting up a banner.

"Dr. Sheldon Minck can't come to the mountain, but the Mountain came to Dr. Minck. Like it?"

"Perfect."

"And under that will be a picture of Mountain, smiling, with a quote signed by him reading, "Dr. Sheldon Minck saved my mouth. He can do the same for you."

"You'll be turning patients away," I said.

"Think so?"

"Can't miss," I said.

"The guy with the great teeth is in your office," he said.

"Violet told me," I said.

"She tell you I lost five dollars to her on some boxing match?"

"No, but it doesn't surprise me. You want some advice, Shel? Don't bet against Violet on any sport, and don't even think about putting a hand on her. Rocky will come back some day and maybe not in the very distant future."

Shelly nodded glumly.

"Do we really need a receptionist?" he asked.

"Absolutely," I said.

"Then how about you kicking in a few dollars for her salary? She takes messages for both of us."

"Fair enough," I said. "How about a dollar a month?"

"Well . . ."

"Seventy-five cents?"

"A dollar," he said.

I went into my office while he pushed his glasses back on his nose and thought about his imaginary giant ad.

Cary Grant was standing at the window with his hands in his pockets. He turned when I came in.

"Who are those people down there?" he asked.

He had been looking down at the rubble of the small empty lot behind the Farraday with its two decaying automobile wrecks and a little cardboard shack.

"Winos, a few crazies, once in a while, people just down on their luck," I said.

"What must it be like?" he asked.

"I try not to think about it very much," I said, standing across from him.

"Does it work? Not thinking about it?"

"Most of the time," I said.

Grant let out a deep sigh and said, "Look, I'm sorry about last night, walking out on you. Believe me I had to. I made some calls and got you and the others out."

"And the Nazis, don't forget them," I said.

"I'm not. They were let go so they could be watched."

"To lead them to the big trout," I said.

"Big trout?"

"Figure of speech," I said. "The head man."

"Right. But it probably won't work. They'll all be too careful. Besides, there wasn't enough evidence of anything to hold them. The FBI is checking their fingerprints now, but I doubt if they'll come up with anything."

"So?"

He circled around the desk, his head down, thinking.

"He'll probably try to run," Grant said. "Get out of the country, make his way to South America or Canada and then maybe back to Germany. The people I'm working with have good rea sons for thinking he has some important information, possibly that list of names Volkman was trying to sell me, perhaps even more names."

"You mean British Intelligence?" I said, sitting in the chair closest to my Dalí painting.

"They do have fewer constraints than your FBI," he agreed.

"Meaning they'd kill our man if they found him?"

"Possibly," Grant said, scratching his ear and not facing me. "Possibly."

"So what's your plan?"

"We flush him out," Grant said.

"With what?"

"The transcriptions," he said. "The ones Volkman and Cookinham made."

"We're not sure . . ."

"We don't have to be," Grant said. "He has to think they exist and that we have them, or rather he has to think you have them. He wouldn't believe I'd try to blackmail him."

"How do we do this?" I asked.

"Simple," he said. "You see Miss Jacklyn Wright and tell her you want to make a deal for the transcriptions. You can't call her. Her phone will be tapped."

"If I go near her, the FBI will pick me up," I said.

"Right," Grant said, pacing in the small space next to my desk, one hand in a pocket, the other rubbing the back of his head. "Is there anyone you can send who the FBI won't recognize from last night?"

"Maybe," I said.

"Who?"

"Sheldon Minck," I said.

From beyond the door came Shelly's voice singing, "Give me some men who are stout-hearted men."

Grant stopped pacing and tilted his head to one side to look at me as if I were a bizarre specimen.

"I'm sorry if he's your friend," Grant said. "But from what I've seen of that man, I think he represents a distinct threat to society."

"He can do it," I said. "He can make it casual, slip her a note saying, 'I've got the transcriptions. Tell him.' And sign it 'Peters.'"

"He won't talk to her?" Grant asked.

"I'll tell him not to."

"Will he listen?"

"Probably."

"Do we have a choice?"

"Not a good one I can think of right now," I said.

Grant faced me, clasped his hands, and put his knuckles to his mouth.

"All right," he said. "When?"

"Right away," I said. "I'll write the note, put it in an envelope, send Shelly to Caroll College, tell him to give it to the secretary in the School of Performance for Jacklyn Wright and turn around and walk away."

Grant nodded. He didn't have much enthusiasm for the plan but was going to go along with it. I found a reasonably unblemished sheet of paper in my desk drawer and a pencil that wasn't too blunt. I wrote the note, put it in an envelope, then sealed it without writing Jacklyn Wright's name on it.

When Grant and I went back into Shelly's office, he was still alone. He grinned at us.

"You've got a patient coming?" I asked.

"Not for a few hours," Shelly said. "I'm going to work on my ad campaign."

"You said you wanted to help. I've got a job for you. If you hurry, you can get it done and be back before your patient arrives."

"It's important?"

"Yes."

"Spy stuff?" he asked.

"Yes," I said.

Shelly looked at Grant and then at me.

"I'm your man."

I told him what to do and handed him the envelope. He took off his smock, put on his jacket, and stuck the envelope in his pocket.

"Remember," Grant said. "Don't say anything to anyone but the secretary. All you say to her is 'Please give this to Miss Wright,' and then you turn around and come back here."

"Can do," Shelly said. "What's it about?"

"Can't tell you, Shel," I said. "For your own good."

"Gotcha," Sheldon said, winked at Grant and said, in probably the worst imitation I had ever heard, "Judy, Judy, Judy. I know who you are."

Grant smiled uncomfortably.

When Shelly was out of the door, I looked at Grant.

"I never said Judy, Judy, Judy in a movie," he said. "In *Only Angels Have Wings*, Rita Hayworth played a character named Judy. I had lines like 'Come on Judy' and 'Hello Judy' and 'Now, now Judy', but never 'Judy, Judy, Judy.' That was invented by some comedian named Storch when he introduced Judy Garland at a show. I think more people say that to me than 'hello.' I have to tell you, Peters, I don't have a great deal of faith in your dentist friend."

"How much damage can he do?" I asked.

"The human mind can only begin to contemplate the possibilities," Grant said. "What now?"

"We wait," I said.

CHAPTER 13

"WE'RE HAVING DINNER for a few friends tonight," Grant said, checking his watch as he sat in Shelly's dental chair. "Regular group. Freddy Brisson and Roz Russell, Gene Tierney and Oleg Casini, Louis Jourdan and his wife, Alex Korda and Merle Oberon, and June Duprez and the Baron Guy de Rothschild."

"Impressive," I said.

"It was meant to impress," he said. "The point is I've got to be there. Let's just say relations between me and my wife are getting a little strained. If I missed this dinner, I don't know what would happen."

"Does she know about you and British Intelligence?" I asked.

"No, and she's not going to. I probably shouldn't have told you, but I've almost gotten you killed. I still might manage to do that. You deserve to know what you're in for."

I nodded and leaned against the wall. Grant kept checking his watch.

"Another strain on my marriage is that I'm on the board of the

Hollywood Victory Committee, the clearinghouse for all movie talent for servicemen shows. I'm also on the board of the United Nations War Relief and the Jesterate of Masquers, a theatrical group that puts on shows for war workers. In short, I'm not home very much. What's keeping him?"

"He'll be, . . . " I began, and Shelly burst into the room panting.

"Ran . . . up . . . the . . . stairs," he said, holding his chest. "Need . . . to . . . sit."

Grant got up and Shelly moved to the dental chair, where he immediately pulled out and lit a fresh cigar, which did nothing to help him catch his breath.

"What happened?" Grant asked.

"A . . . minute," Shelly said breathing deeply.

Grant looked at me.

"Shel, just nod if you delivered the envelope."

Shelly nodded.

"Any problems?"

He shook his head "no."

"Do you know if the secretary delivered the envelope?"

He nodded.

"Good. You delivered it and left."

"Yes," he got out.

"It's done," I said to Grant.

"Now you're the target," Grant said. "I should be here with you. Maybe after the dinner. . . ."

"I'll be fine," I said. "If he contacts me, I'll call you."

"Right," said Grant, moving toward the door. "And, thanks, Dr. Minck."

Shelly, still having trouble getting his breath, waved a hand to show his acceptance. When Grant was gone, Shelly finally stopped panting and said, "Teeth need work."

"His teeth are fine," I said.

"Not his, hers, the secretary at Caroll College."

"Don't tell me what you're going to tell me, Shel," I said.

"Tell you what? The woman needs work. I told her I was a dentist and gave her a card. She said she would call me."

I decided not to tell him what identifying himself to the woman might mean to his general future well-being. There was a knock at the door to the reception area. Shelly took the cigar from his mouth and called, "Come in."

A very tiny woman who couldn't have weighed more than eighty pounds came in, anxiously clutching a purse to her chest. Her hair was a badly dyed brown, and her eyes were wide with fear as she looked around the dental office.

"Mrs. Andropropov," Shelly said. "You're right on time."

Shelly put on his smock while I looked at Mrs. Andropropov, who looked at me as if I might have an answer to some question she was having trouble forming.

"Have a seat," Sheldon said.

The woman took small steps toward the chair and climbed in, still clutching her purse.

"Heard of Mountain, the wrestler?" he asked her as he prepared her for the reign of terror.

She shook her head "no."

"He's a good friend of mine," said Sheldon. "A patient. I saved his smile. I'm going to save yours too."

So far, I had seen no smile on Mrs. Andropropov. I went quietly to my office as Shelly began examining the tools laid out on the table next to the chair. He started humming "Listen to the Mockingbird." By the time I was back in my office with the door closed, I could hear him singing as the whirring of his drill began, with its familiar skip every four or five seconds.

The phone started ringing when I got into the chair behind my desk.

"Gunther," Violet said.

Gunther came on the line.

"Toby, I have some information on Caroll College."

"Go on."

"The president of the college is a man named Hans Uberfeldt, born in Austria, degrees in mathematics and science from Heidelberg University. Family is still in Germany. There is nothing, however, to indicate that he is anything but a loyal citizen of the United States, but . . ."

"He deserves a closer look," I said.

"I shall do that."

"Anything else?"

"No ties yet that I can find, but I'll continue to look. The provost is Alexander Jackson Hamilton. Family dates back to before your Revolutionary War. Chairman of the college War Bond drive, which has been very successful."

"Who hired Jacklyn Wright?" I said.

"I don't know, but I shall endeavor to find out," said Gunther. "I am in search of members of the senior faculty and the dean of the School of Performance, who's on leave to work on a book on exercises in voice projection. One more piece of information on Dr. Hamilton. It could not have been he who hired Miss Wright. When she was given her present position three years ago, Dr. Hamilton was a full professor of mathematics at Middlebury College."

"Model citizen," I said.

"So it would seem."

"President Uberfeldt might be our man," I said.

"I have not checked out others on the administration, faculty, and staff," said Gunther. "I will begin to do so. Toby, is it not likely that whoever you seek has nothing to do with Caroll College?"

"Very likely," I said, "but I don't know where else to look."

"I shall continue," Gunther said.

He hung up and I sat looking at the phone. I wasn't sure if I was going to get a call, a knock at the door, a bullet in the stomach, or nothing but silence. After an hour of listening to Mrs. Andropropov moaning low and Shelly singing, I started to get up.

The phone rang again.

"Anita," Violet announced. Anita came on.

"You getting anywhere?" she asked.

"Two dead men so far and a den of Nazis," I said.

"And?"

"Nothing I can talk about over the phone. You working?"

"I'm working till ten," she said.

"I think I'll come by for some chili and sympathy."

"How're your neck and head?"

"Better. Could be even better than that. Could also be worse."

I drove to the Regal drugstore and found a parking spot with no trouble. When I went in, I picked up another bottle of Bayer aspirin tablets, paid the cashier, opened the bottle, and downed three with a quick gulp.

When I moved to the lunch counter, Anita was serving a man in overalls. A pair of work gloves hung out of his back pocket, and a fading tattoo of a mermaid danced on his hairy forearm. The man said something. Anita poured him some coffee and laughed. Then she spotted me and came over.

"You look bouncy this morning," I said.

"Guess I am. My daughter's away for a week. War news is good. I'm getting a raise and I bought myself a new dress, a rayon print for $3.98 at Macy's. I'll wear it to the movies tonight."

"Let's make that Friday," I said. "I have to save the United States from Nazis for the next couple of days."

Anita nodded.

"Friday, fine," she said. "But I pick the movie. *Princess O'Rourke* with Olivia deHavilland, Robert Cummings, and Jane Wyman."

"I can live with that," I said.

"Dinner first."

"I can pay for that," I said.

"Can I get you something?"

"Coffee," I said. " Chili. Spicy. I just had Trout Plaut. Trout baked in peanut butter. Can't get rid of the taste."

Anita poured me a mug of coffee and brought me a bowl of chili with a package of oyster crackers. I crumbled the crackers into the chili.

"Look at this," said the man in the overalls, looking at his newspaper as he ate. "Dorothy Lamour toured war plants in Cleveland, and the women unionists named her a war hazard. Said she took the men away from the assembly line. Can you beat that? She comes to our place, and I damn guarantee you production goes way up—and not just production. Can you beat that?"

I couldn't, so I drank my coffee. It was hot and strong. I ate my chili. It was spicy and helped me forget Trout Plaut.

A couple came in and sat on stools side-by-side between me and the man in overalls. They were young. He was a soldier in khakis, PFC. She had curly red hair cut short. They looked like they had just come from posing for a magazine ad to raise money for the savings bonds.

"Hungry?" he asked, touching her hand.

"Starving," she answered, looking into his eyes.

She caught me looking their way and the young woman said, "We were married yesterday at Immanuel Presbyterian Church on Wilshire."

She held up her left hand to show her ring.

"Beautiful," Anita said.

"Perfect," I said.

The man in the overalls said nothing. The couple ordered, and I drank coffee and finished my chili. A man in a dark suit and tie came in and sat down a few seats to my left. He was about forty and had a serious face. I looked at him. He didn't look back. I looked at him in the mirror over the milkshake mixer. He didn't meet my eyes there, either. He sat with his hands in his lap till Anita came to take his order. Coffee and toast.

Anita came back to me with a refill, and I whispered, "You know that guy?"

"Never saw him before," she said, starting to turn her head to look at him.

"Don't look his way," I said.

"Who is he?" she asked.

"Probably just a customer," I said.

Anita moved to work on the young couple's order, and I tried again without success to get the man in the suit to meet my eyes in the mirror. He could have just been street trade. He could have been a cop or an FBI agent on my tail. He could have been a Nazi. He could have been working himself up to approach me and try to save my soul or sell me a vacuum cleaner.

I was almost through with a second cup of coffee. I was feeling a little better. Either the aspirin had kicked in, or the coffee had, or both.

The young soldier asked, "Restroom?"

Anita pointed to the back of the store. He thanked her and touched the young woman's cheek. She took his hand and put her lips to it before letting it go.

"Young love," said Anita to me as the soldier walked toward the restroom.

"It'll last forever," I said.

"Or till he ships out and leaves her alone," said Anita. Then she recovered and with a sigh said, "Sorry."

"Excused."

The young woman smiled at us and dug into a plate of bacon, eggs, and fried potatoes. She had an appetite. A few seconds later the soldier was back.

"Excuse me," he said to me. "I knocked at the door. Nobody answered. I think it's stuck. Can you give me a hand?"

"Sure," I said, downing what remained of the coffee in the cup.

I got off the stool and followed him to the rear of the drugstore. The door to the bathroom, which I had used many times before, was closed.

"It gets stuck sometimes," I said, reaching for the handle. I turned it and it opened without a problem.

I looked at the soldier, who said, "Thanks. That door leads to the outside?" he asked, nodding at the delivery entrance next to the restroom.

"Yes," I said.

"Let's go out."

Since he had a gun in his hand complete with a large silencer, I decided to do what he said. He stayed a safe yard behind me as I unlocked the service entrance and stepped outside.

"What about your wife?" I asked.

"By now she's told your lady friend that she forgot something in the car and has left, saying she'll be right back."

There was a dark four-door Dodge with tinted windows parked just outside the door.

"Wait," he said.

We stood there. The young red-haired woman who had said she was his wife came running around a corner toward us.

"Open the passenger door," the soldier said to me. "And leave the door open."

I did. The woman was with us now. When I had the door open, she patted me down for a weapon. My .38 was in the glove compartment of my Crosley on the other side of the building. There were times I would have salvaged a small amount of pleasure from being patted down by a pretty young woman. This wasn't one of them.

The soldier handed the young woman his gun, and she stepped back to be a safe distance away from me. He went around to the driver's side, got in, and closed the door.

"Get in," she said, keeping the gun on me. "And don't close the door."

I got in and she kept the gun on me as she got into the backseat.

"Now close your door," she said as she closed hers.

I closed my door.

"I have my gun pointed at your neck," she said. "Sit quietly. I have orders to shoot you if I even suspect that you might be making a move."

The soldier made a tight circle in the little delivery lot and aimed the car for the street. In the rearview mirror, I could see the drugstore delivery door fly open. The well-dressed man who had refused to meet my eyes came out, gun in hand, saw us, and leveled his weapon in our direction.

"He won't shoot," the soldier said.

And he didn't. Instead, the man with the gun ran back into the drugstore.

"By the time he gets to his car," the soldier said, "he'll have no idea which way we are going."

"Which way are we going?"

"To a place where none but those who do what they are told ever leave," the young woman said.

I looked at her in the rearview mirror. She was smiling again, but it was a very different smile from the one she had given the soldier at the counter. It was the smile of a person who knew something I didn't know.

We drove west in silence down El Segundo toward the ocean. About half a mile before we hit Highland, he turned down a small neighborhood street with few cars parked, lots of trees, and small houses with neat lawns with about fifty feet between them. We pulled into the driveway of one of the houses, where a woman in a dark dress, her hair pulled back in a bun opened the garage door. We drove in. The woman in the dark dress closed the garage behind us.

The soldier got out, and I reached for the handle.

"Wait," the woman in the backseat said.

I waited till the soldier had come around and opened my door.

"Now," the woman said.

I got out. The garage was empty, not a tool, not a can of paint. Shelves were empty. There were a few cobwebs in the corners. A single lightbulb was on overhead. There were no windows.

"Through there," the soldier said, pointing to a door.

I opened the door and found myself in a kitchen that looked as bare as the garage. Dust danced in the sunbeam from the window over the sink.

"Come," the soldier said.

I followed him through another empty room. This one had white walls and blue carpet. It looked as if it might be a dining room. There was no furniture. The soldier kept leading the way with the two women behind us. We walked into another blue carpeted room with big windows facing the street. There were shades on the windows and the shades were down. Some light was getting through and a small cheap-looking chandelier with about a dozen lights was on.

There were two chairs in this room, wooden folding chairs facing each other.

"Sit," said the soldier.

I picked a chair and sat. The women stayed behind me. The soldier took up a position in front of me with his hands folded in front of him.

Something was making a clacking noise in the room behind him, and a man emerged carrying two glasses of something dark with ice cubes. I recognized the man. He was the cop who had rousted me from Elysian Park, only now he wore blue slacks and a white short-sleeved pullover shirt with a soft collar and the words "Washington Yacht Club" stitched in blue on the pocket over his heart.

He handed me a drink.

"Pepsi with ice, right?" he said pleasantly.

"Thanks," I said, taking the drink.

"I'm drinking something a bit more potent," he said, sitting in the other folding chair across from me. He hitched up his pants leg and held up his glass.

"Cheers," he said.

I held up my Pepsi.

"How about them?" I asked, nodding at the other three in the room.

"Ah, this is a business drink," the man in the chair said. "And we are about to have a business meeting."

"Nice house you have here," I said, taking a sip of Pepsi.

"It's an unoccupied house for sale," the man said, looking around. "Simple, undistinctive, quiet. We won't be disturbed."

I didn't speak. I drank my Pepsi and waited while he took manly gulps of whatever it was he was downing.

"Let's talk," he said.

"Let's," I agreed.

"You have some transcriptions made by Volkman and Cookinham," he said.

"Not on me."

"Obviously," he said. "They would take some space."

I didn't answer. I drank.

"What is it you want in exchange for those transcriptions?" he asked. "I mean, what do you want in addition to your life?"

"One hundred and twelve thousand dollars," I said.

The man paused with his drink almost to his lips and said, "How do you come up with such a precise figure?"

"Don't know," I said. "Just came to mind."

"You have a strange sense of humor," he said, looking at the soldier, who wore no expression. "And you're not afraid?"

"Oh, I'm afraid," I said. "I'm just good at not showing it, and I know you won't kill me as long as you don't have those transcriptions."

"Or as long as we believe that they exist and you do have them," he said.

"They exist," I said.

"Actually, I know," he said.

He nodded at the soldier, who nodded back and moved into the room from which the man across from me had come. He was back in about ten seconds with a thick folder, which he handed to the man in the chair.

"These are the typed versions of those transcriptions," he said. "We found them hidden in Volkman's apartment when we brought his body there. They are very compromising."

"Lots of names, places, plans," I said.

"I take it you haven't listened to the recordings," he said.

"No."

"Good. For the moment I'll trust you on that. If you have listened to them and taken notes, I . . . well, you understand."

"Perfectly," I said. "But I know where they are, and I want one hundred and twelve thousand and fifty dollars."

"And fifty dollars?"

"My hourly rate for Nazis," I said.

The man tried to hide a smile and then decided not to. He let out a small laugh.

"The faster we get this done," I said. "The less it costs you."

"It will take me a few hours to get that kind of cash," he said.

"Add on fifty dollars for every hour we wait," I said.

"Get the money," the man said, looking over my shoulder.

I heard someone move behind me and watched the woman with the bun who had opened the garage door move back toward the kitchen. A minute later, I heard the garage door open and the Dodge back out.

"When you have the money," the man said, "you tell us where the transcriptions are. We get them and we let you go."

"And you let me go?"

"Yes."

"Why?" I asked.

He laughed.

"You're right," he said, and then to the soldier, "He's right. Well, Mr. Peters, what do you propose?"

"Let me think about it," I said.

"Another Pepsi?"

"Sure."

The man nodded. The soldier took my glass and headed for the room where the drinks were.

"You have a name I can use?" I asked.

"Many," the man said. "How about 'Joe'? Mundane. Easy to remember, but not a name I would like to use for a prolonged period."

"Joe," I said. "You're not an American, are you?"

"I am not," he said. "And I am. I have citizenship, but that is . . ."

He waved it away with his hand.

"You're not going to try something stupid are you?" he asked.

"I'm not planning to," I lied.

"It would be a mistake," he said as the soldier returned with another Pepsi for me and another drink for Joe. "You have a sister-in-law named Ruth, your brother's wife, the mother of your two nephews."

I didn't answer.

"She is dying," he said sadly. "Maybe with all that money you could find some doctor in New York or someplace who could help her. I know of a specialist in Santiago, Chile, who could help her."

"You know what's wrong with her?" I asked.

"Yes," he said. "You are a vulnerable man, Peters. Your family is vulnerable, as are your freakish friends and your former wife, for whom I understand you have a great affection. Anne is her name?"

"Yes," I said.

"And the waitress at the drugstore where we followed you. Anita?"

"You're very well informed."

"And generous," he said. "I could simply threaten the lives of all of them if you don't give me the transcriptions, but I don't like to work that way. There are, I admit, barbarians on our side who seem to delight in the pain and suffering of others. For me, it is the last resort."

"So," I said, "you killed Volkman and Cookinham?"

"Volkman, no. My associate . . ." He looked at the young man in the uniform, "who we shall simply call 'Soldier' did the shooting. I knocked you out. He removed the body and I, in my ill-fitting police uniform, successfully got rid of you."

"Why didn't you kill me?" I asked.

"Is that a wise question to plant in my mind?"

"I'm pretty sure it was already there."

"Well," he said. "The only thing Volkman said to you was

'George Hall,' and I was confident it would have no meaning, that you would go off on a wild duck race."

"Goose chase," I corrected.

"I don't like cliches," Joe said, recrossing his legs and checking his watch.

I could sense the young redheaded girl with the gun behind me, but I had to give her credit: not a move, shift, or loud breath.

"And," Joe went on, "it was nice to have you to throw to the police and the FBI for the murder. It kept them busy."

"I need the toilet," I said, holding up my finished second Pepsi.

"Through there," he said, looking over his shoulder. "Miss Jones will accompany you. There is no window in the lavatory, and she will most certainly shoot you if you attempt to escape."

"Then you won't get your transcriptions," I said.

His sigh was deep.

"If you try to escape, it will suggest strongly that you have no intention of turning them over or that you do not have them."

I got up. There was no way they were going to let me get out of this alive, especially when they found out that I had no idea where the transcriptions were. I walked across the room and looked back over my shoulder at Miss Jones, who was a safe distance behind me.

The bathroom was inside a bedroom furnished only with a metal cooler with a set of glasses on top of it. I went into the bathroom and closed the door.

The medicine cabinet was empty. I unscrewed the metal showerhead and looked at the toilet.

"There's no toilet paper," I called through the closed door.

"There is no toilet paper," she called into the next room.

I stood in the space next to the door, backed against the toilet roll bar, the heavy showerhead in my hand. Less than a minute later, I heard Soldier say, "Here are some napkins."

I opened the door and he put his hand in to give me a small stack of napkins. I yanked him in, kicked the door shut, shoved his face into the toilet bowel tank, and locked the door.

A shot came through the door, making a hole a few inches from my hand.

"I'm holding Soldier against the door," I shouted. "You missed him, but you'll probably get him with the next shot."

Soldier was slumped over the toilet, facedown, not quite out but not quite alert either. I banged his head on the edge of the toilet for good luck and went through his pockets. There was a gun—a Walther—not my weapon of choice, but nothing is.

I heard talking outside the door. I climbed into the bathtub and ducked. Then Joe called, "Peters, this is absurd. You can't get out of there."

"And you can't get in."

"We can simply shoot through the door till we kill you," he said. "I can only gather from this that you don't know where the transcriptions are."

"I know," I said. "But I don't trust you."

"The money will be here shortly," he said. "Think of your brother's wife. Consider what could happen to your family and friends."

"Here's my deal," I said. "You go back in the other room. I come out with Soldier in front of me. Miss Jones puts down her gun, and when the money comes, we deal."

"That does not sound acceptable," Joe said.

"Okay," I said. "Try this. You go in the other room. I come out, tell you where the transcriptions are and give you Soldier. Then I walk out the front door with no money."

There was silence while he considered my offer.

"No," he said.

"You could get shot," I said.

"I wouldn't like that," said Joe. "I wouldn't like that at all."

"Soldier would definitely get shot," I said.

"He is a soldier," said Joe. "Soldiers get shot in time of war. Very well. Miss Jones and I are moving into the living room."

I hoped a neighbor had heard Miss Jones's shot through the bathroom door, but I wasn't about to count on it. Unfortunately, as I had seen, she had the silencer on. I counted to fifteen and looked down at Soldier, who had a large purple lump over his left eye. He seemed to be dreaming, probably about Berlin or a warm bath.

I opened the door slowly. There was no one in the bedroom. I kept my eye on the door to the living room and stayed close to the wall.

"I'm out," I said.

"Join us," Joe said.

"I think I'll stay here."

"I believe I hear Miss Smith returning with your money," he said. "We are out of time."

"Okay," I said. "Put the money down by the garage door. I'll come out, tell you where the transcriptions are, and go through the garage. Tell Miss Smith to leave the garage door open and the keys in the car."

"I will do so," said Joe.

"Fine."

I heard the door from the garage open and heard voices.

"It's done," Joe said. "The moment of *verité* is upon us, Mr. Peters. Fate, *Shiksahl* in German, now enters the game.

"All of you in the kitchen," I said. "Guns on the counter. I'll take you with me, Joe."

"Can't have that," Joe said. "You'll have to shoot me if that's your only plan, and then you would surely be dead."

"Fine, I'll take Miss Jones."

"That can be arranged."

I gave them time to move into the kitchen and eased out of the bedroom door carefully, gun leveled toward where they would be. They were there. Miss Jones and Miss Smith both had weapons in their hands. Joe stood behind them, a closed cardboard box on the floor in front of him.

"Miss Jones puts her gun down now," I said.

"Do it," said Joe.

She did. Now I did what Joe might consider the stupid thing I was considering.

"The transcriptions are hidden among the record albums in Cookinham's house," I improvised. "He pulled out the real records, threw them away and replaced them with transcriptions, hid them in plain sight."

"That sounds like our Mr. Cookinham," Joe said.

I stepped forward in their direction and then to the right, just out of their line of vision. I ran to the front door, opened it, and ran out toward the street. The hell with the money, the hostage, and the car. I was sure they counted on me wanting that money. I was sure Joe had worked out a way to kill me before I got out of the garage. At least, I was sure enough to run out into the street and move like hell toward the next house.

It took them a few seconds to figure out what I had done. By the time they got to the front door and Miss Jones and Miss Smith could raise their weapons and fire, I had made it around the side of the house next door.

They each fired once. Miss Smith's weapon had no silencer. Anyone in the neighborhood was now either hiding or on their phone to the police. Behind the house I had run around was a line of bushes. I ran headlong into the bushes, cut my arms, pants, face, and shirt but didn't let go of the Walther. When I got to the other side of the hedge, I knelt down, turned, and aimed toward where they would be coming from—if they were coming.

But they didn't. I heard a car, probably the Dodge in the garage, and watching the gap between the two houses in front of me, I saw it drive toward El Segunda.

Ten minutes later, I found a phone booth on El Segunda, pulled change out of my pocket, and called Mrs. Plaut's. She answered.

"It's me, Mr. Peters," I shouted.

A woman with her hair coming undone while she tried to keep from dropping an overloaded and oversized brown paper bag full of groceries shifted the load as she passed the phone booth. The look she gave me told me that I should find a mirror. A finger to my cheek told me I was bleeding from my dash through the bushes.

"Mrs. Plaut?"

"Yes."

"It's me, Toby Peters."

"Yes, it's you, Mr. Peelers."

"Is Mr. Wherthman there?"

"They are," she said.

"They?"

"Mr. Gunther and the other men," she said.

"What other men?"

"You'll have to ask Mr. Gunther."

She put the phone down and I tried to call her back with a loud, "Wait, Mrs. Plaut."

I heard shuffling, the phone being lifted, and Gunther's voice.

"Toby?"

"Yes, what's going on? Who's there?"

"They want . . . " Gunther began and someone took the phone from him."

"Peters?"

"Yes."

I recognized the voice of FBI Agent Cantwell.

"Where are you? Where have you been and who were those people you took off with?"

"I'm at a phone booth on El Segunda. I've been in a house near here that's for sale, though unless its a real steal, I wouldn't recommend it. The shower is broken. There are bullet holes in one of the doors and blood on the bathroom floor."

"An address."

I described the house and the street. I hadn't looked at the address.

"Get someone to Cookinham's house," I said.

"Why?"

"I told them there was something they wanted there," I said. "If you hurry, you might beat them there or catch them carting out the record albums."

"Record albums?"

"I told them Cookinham's record albums were filled with transcriptions Volkman and Cookinham had made of their meetings."

"Are they?" asked Cantwell.

"No," I said. "But they'll check."

"Where exactly are you?"

I looked up at the street sign and told him.

"Stay there. Someone will pick you up in ten minutes."

He hung up. There was a cigar store near the phone booth. I went in, bought a package of Kleenex, and asked if I could use the restroom.

The lumpy man behind the counter nodded toward the back of the shop, where I found the tiny bathroom. The mirror could have used a cleaning, but I could see enough to tell me that my jacket was torn, my face had two bleeding scratches, and my hair stuck up like Stan Laurel's.

I did my best to clean up. It couldn't have been more than three or four minutes later that I walked out of the cigar store. A dark car was parked at the curb, and two very serious-looking men in dark suits were standing on the sidewalk looking at me.

"Identification," I said, my hand in my pocket on the Walther.

Both FBI agents pulled out their wallets and showed cards. A few people walking by looked at us but no one stopped. I stepped forward and looked at their cards. They might be fake, but they looked real to me and I didn't have much choice. One of them patted me down and took the Walther. Then he opened the back door of the car and got in beside me. The other drove.

Ten minutes later we were in the interrogation room of the Wilshire Police Department. With me were Cantwell and his partner, D'Argentero and my brother, Phil. They stood. I sat.

"Now," said Cantwell. "Tell us what happened."

CHAPTER 14

I TOLD THEM the story, displayed my wounds, and told them how to get to the house I had escaped from. The agent named D'Argentero took notes quietly. My brother stood back against the wall, arms folded, looking angry. I didn't try to guess who Phil was angry with. It could be me, the FBI, the Nazis, some criminal, or himself. Phil had perfected the art of anger and he could become very creative with it when he let it out.

"Okay," said Cantwell when I finished. "We . . ."

There was a knock at the door, to the small room and then the man who had been at the drugstore lunch counter and followed me and my kidnappers into the alley stepped in. He didn't bother to look at me.

"All the record albums are missing from Cookinham's house," he said.

"They work fast," said Cantwell. "Thanks."

The man from the drugstore left.

"You've got the Nazis from the college," Phil burst out. "Bring them in. Pick out the toughest and give me fifteen minutes with him. You'll have all your questions answered."

"We don't work like that, Lieutenant," Cantwell said calmly.

"Like hell you don't," Phil said.

"We need this person who called himself 'Joe,'" said Cantwell. We need to find him and take him before he gets away. He's the fish. The others are minnows."

"With sharp teeth," Phil said. He stormed out of the room.

"Your brother has a temper," Cantwell said.

"I've noticed."

"How about you? You don't seem to have a temper."

"Haven't spent much time thinking about it, but you may be right," I said.

The agent from the drugstore came in again. He handed a sheet of paper to Cantwell, who took the seat across from me at the table.

"We just got a call," he said. "Found the house. Broken showerhead, bullet holes, a cooler with melted ice with some glasses we might be able to get prints off of, and blood in the bathroom."

This was support for my story, but Cantwell had a look on his face that said there was a marble or two more to drop.

"You say you took that Walther from this man dressed like a soldier?"

"That's right," I said.

"Right," said Cantwell. "It's not your gun."

"I've got a thirty-eight, registered, in the glove compartment of my car."

"Not the best place to keep a gun," he said.

"I don't have a lot of choices."

"So the first time you saw the Walther was an hour or so ago when you took it from a man dressed like a soldier."

"A PFC," I said.

"And there was a man named Joe and two women named Smith and Jones?"

"I don't think those were their real names," I said helpfully.

"We considered that," he said somberly. "Peters, we just did a quick ballistics check. We'll need to examine the gun and the bullets more carefully, but we're reasonably sure the Walther was used to kill Volkman."

"I told you . . ."

Cantwell held up his hand to stop me.

"It gets worse," he said. "We called your office a few minutes ago, talked to a Dr. Minck."

I had a feeling I was about to hear something I did not want to hear.

"He had a message for you," Cantwell said. "Someone had called and asked him to write it down. Have any idea what it said, this message?"

"None," I said shifting on the hard chair.

"It was from someone who called himself Joe," said Cantwell. "Joe wanted you to know that he had found what he was looking for exactly where you said it would be and that he was pleased he had not disposed of you."

Cantwell folded his hands on the table and looked at me, waiting for a reaction. D'Argentero stood next to him, his eyes on my face.

"The transcriptions really *were* in those albums?" I said.

"That would seem a logical conclusion," said Cantwell. "So, what do we make of all this? You have a gun that killed one of two blackmailers who were making transcriptions of Nazi meetings. You knew where the transcriptions were. You gave this information to Nazis."

"Now wait . . ."

"Look at it from where I sit, Peters. It wouldn't take a great leap of imagination to come to the conclusion that you learned about the transcriptions, killed Volkman and Cookinham, and then sold the transcriptions to the Nazis."

"Why would I keep the murder weapon?"

Cantwell leaned forward and spoke as if he were sharing a secret, "Because you are not the brightest bulb in the chandelier and you're burning out fast."

"I want to call my lawyer," I said.

"No need," said Cantwell. "We're not going to hold you. We've checked your history. You're dumb but reasonably honest, and there's nothing in your jacket that suggests you'd do something like this. We could be wrong, but we see you as the poor sap who got caught in the middle and tripped us when we tried to get by and put our hands on the bad guys."

"So what now?" I asked.

"Go," said Cantwell.

"Just 'go'?" I asked.

"Unless you want to stick around and discuss the war. Seen the papers today? We shot down seventeen Japanese planes, sunk two freighters and a cruiser, and the marines are moving forward fast in New Britain."

"That's great," I said.

"And Pappy Boyington got his twenty-sixth kill," D'Argentero added.

"Agent D'Argentero's brother's in the Black Sheep Squadron," Cantwell explained.

I moved to the door.

"One last thing, Peters," Cantwell said as I started out. "Stay out of our way and tell your client to sit this one out."

I nodded and moved into the squad room. It was reasonably full of perps, suspects, witnesses, pleading, moaning, whining, coughing, and cops getting angry, talking on phones, or filling in reports. Phil stood at his office door with a cup of coffee in his hands. He was looking at me. It struck me that his gut had gotten a little bigger and his suspenders a little wider.

He opened his door, left it open, and went in. I went in after him. He was behind his desk in his chair. I sat across from him.

"They let me go," I said.

"Figures," he said and went silent, looking into his mug. Then he lifted his head and went on. "They, this Joe Nazi, he threatened Ruth, the boys, the baby?"

"He threatened everyone I know," I said.

"I don't care about everyone you know," Phil said tightly. "I care about my family. Did he mean it, the threat?"

"He's a Nazi," I said. "Probably."

"You know that even if you got that one hundred thousand, it wouldn't have saved Ruth. There's nothing that can save her," he said, starting to turn his mug slowly on the desk. It would definitely leave a new ring to join the dozens of others.

"I know," I said.

"I want to find your friend Joe," Phil said.

I nodded and waited for him to say something else.

He didn't, just kept turning his coffee mug. I got up.

"You find him, you call me first," he said, looking up at me. "Your word."

"My word," I said.

"Freddy'll drive you to your car," he said.

I said thanks and walked into the squad room. Freddy was patrolman Freddy Sanbucco. Freddy had a bad right leg and a left shoulder that kept him from moving his arm higher than his chest. Both the leg and shoulder were five-year-old hits from the gun of a woman who had been holding her husband at bay in the couple's small apartment. The husband had no shirt on and a hairy chest. He was also holding a meat cleaver. Freddy remembered both the cleaver and the hairy chest vividly.

Freddy had stepped in and told the wife that the situation was under control now.

"You're going to take him away?" the woman had asked.

"I am," Freddy had said.

"But he'll come back," she had said hysterically.

"That's up to a judge," Freddy said, holding out his left hand for the cleaver and gun. His own weapon was in his right hand.

"He'll come back and kill me," she had said.

Looking at the husband, Freddy concluded that she might very well be right, but the possibility never came to a test. The woman started firing. Hit her husband in the neck and Freddy in the leg and shoulder. The husband died. Freddy never really recovered. The department kept him on, covered for him at the annual checkups, put him in charge of the records room and running errands.

I was Freddy's errand this morning.

"Nazis, huh?" he asked as he drove me in a marked Los Angeles Police car.

"Yeah," I said.

Freddy looked rugged and fit, but if you met his eyes you could see something soft and retreating where there had once been something hard and confident.

"I'd be in the war if it weren't for . . ."

"I know," I said.

"Everybody knows," said Freddy with a shrug as he drove. "Still got almost fourteen years to go till my pension. Fourteen years is a lot."

"Two minutes can be a lot," I said.

"You telling me?" he said with a chuckle. "Ever consider having a partner?"

"Not enough business," I said. "I can't keep myself in pants and pay the car repairs. But if business starts booming, I'll get back to you."

"Maybe I'll go out on my own," he said, more to himself than to me. "I've got good connections."

"Do the math first," I advised.

"Trying to keep away competition?" he asked as we pulled up in front of the drugstore and next to my Crosley.

"I don't think our client lists would overlap," I said, opening the door. "Tell you what. If you do decide to try it, give me a call. We'll have a couple of tacos and I'll tell you some things you should know."

"I'll do that," Freddy said. He drove away.

Anita was on the customer side of the counter, drinking a cup of coffee and looking at a movie magazine. She didn't notice at first as I moved toward her and began to sit. Then she looked up.

"You owe me thirty cents for two cups of coffee and a bowl of chili," she said.

"Let's make it fifty cents," I said. "I feel like a big spender."

She looked at my face and clothes.

"What happened?" she asked.

"Met up with Nazis and rose bushes," I said.

She reached over and touched my cheek.

"I'll give you some peroxide for that. Don't think you can do much to save the jacket and pants."

"I'll charge it to my client," I said.

She moved behind the counter and went for the coffee.

"What kind of pie you have left?"

"Apple, peach, cherry," she said. "Peach is freshest."

"I'll take a slice."

"I should charge you for all of them," she said. "Boss says I should."

"All of them?"

"The soldier and his wife didn't pay."

"They were busy kidnapping me," I said.

"And the guy in the suit who ran out of here with a gun in his hand?"

"FBI," I explained.

"You lead an exciting life, Toby," she said, bringing me the pie and coffee.

"Some days," I said, washing down four aspirin from the bottle in my pocket with the coffee.

"I'm not sure I like it that exciting," Anita said, playing with a loose strand of her dark blonde hair.

"Sure you do," I said. "Otherwise you would have walked out after that night at the airport."

She shrugged her shoulders and said, "I suppose you're right. Are we still on for the movie tomorrow night?"

"Still on," I said, digging into the pie. It was just right. "If something comes up . . ."

"You'll let me know," she said. "Now you owe me two movies."

"Name one," I said.

"*Footlight Glamour* with Blondie and the Bumsteads," she said.

"You're on," I said.

While I finished, Anita told me that after February 2, point-rationing tokens were going to be used instead of paper coupons.

"Company in Cincinnati is turning out twenty million fiber tokens a day," she said. "Can you imagine?"

"Cincinnati? Yes. Fiber tokens? No," I said.

"And listen," Anita went on, leaning forward. "To show you what a crazy world we're living in. An eight-year-old Negro girl gave birth to an eight-pound baby girl. Can you believe that?"

"Yes," I said. "Maybe."

"Both girls are fine," Anita said with a sigh. "And just last night a Santa Claus dummy was stolen from downtown Los Angeles."

"Is there a reward for finding him?" I asked.

"I don't know. Wait a second."

A fire truck went by outside, its bell clanging. The bell started my head throbbing. I touched the back of my head to be sure my stitches were still neatly in place. They were.

Anita came back with a small bottle of peroxide and a roll of cotton. She leaned over the counter to dab at my cuts, the ones she could reach.

"Ever consider another line of work?" she asked as she found a scratch behind my ear.

"Pest control," I said.

"Exterminator?"

"I've got a head start. Mrs. Plaut already thinks I'm in pest control."

"And an editor," she reminded me.

"A man of many talents," I said.

"And bruises," Anita said. "I'd say 'take care of yourself,' but I don't think it would do any good."

It was my turn to touch her cheek.

I finished my pie and coffee, placed two quarters and a dime neatly on the counter, and headed for the door.

I had one stop to make before I headed home. My latest wounds and torn clothes earned me some odd looks while I shopped at a nearby Ralph's, but no one said anything except the young girl at the checkout counter.

"What happened?" she asked.

She was skinny, freckled, straight blonde hair, no makeup, kind of innocent-cute.

"Nazis," I said. "They tried to kill me."

She nodded her head and put on the bland mask she stored for kooks.

"That's too bad," she said, totaling my purchases and bagging them.

"Things like that happen to me," I said.

Behind me a woman waiting to have her groceries added up, kept her distance and pretended to read the contents on a can of soup.

About fifteen minutes later I was in Mrs. Plaut's dinning room.

"You look a mess, Mr. Peelers," she said.

"I'm sorry."

"What happened?"

"Pest control," I said. "Had to go into some treacherous bushes. Those Hun beetles."

She nodded in understanding and unpacked the groceries.

"Steak, oleo, peanut butter, potatoes, and apple jelly," she said. "Total: one dollar and ninety-four cents which means . . ."

I handed her a dollar and six cents change.

"You are a very odd but honest man, Mr. Peelers," she said.

"Thank you."

"Wait."

She disappeared into her living room, and Stillwell started squawking. When she came back, Mrs. Plaut had a large, almost full bottle of brown liquid. She handed it to me.

"Olivia's oleander-and-thick-oil liniment," she said. "Olivia Gracefounder was my aunt. Use it sparingly. Rub it hard."

"Thanks," I said and got up.

"You are welcome. Remember, as the Mister used to say, 'whatever happens the tides will come and go unless the good Lord decides he's had enough.'"

"I'll remember that," I said, heading for the door.

The bird went nuts when I walked through the living room. He said something. I don't know what.

Going up the stairs was getting harder each time I came back to Mrs. Plaut's. I made it to my room, took off my clothes, and examined them to see if there was anything I could salvage. There wasn't, except for my shirt, which had a blotch of something green on it that could probably be cleaned.

In my boxer shorts, I put on my robe and with Olivia's liniment in hand headed for the bathroom, where I showered and washed without too much pain. My shoulder was feeling a lot better, and the scratches looked worse than they felt until I applied Olivia's liniment. I think I howled in pain. Maybe I screamed. There was a knock at the bathroom door and Gunther called out, "Toby, is that you? Are you all right?"

"It's me. I'm all right."

I put the cursed bottle on the back of the toilet and washed off what I could of the liniment from my body, but it still tingled in shock.

"I must talk to you," said Gunther. "I have made a discovery."

"I'll be right out," I said. "I'll get dressed and come to your room."

"You are sure you are? . . . "

"I'm fine," I said. "If you like I'll sing you a chorus of 'I've Got Rhythm.'"

"That will not be necessary," said Gunther on the other side of the door. "I will see you in my room."

I put on my robe, grabbed the lethal bottle to keep it from falling into innocent hands, and went back to my room, where I put on a pair of blue slacks that could have used a little pressing and maybe even a cleaning. In the back of the closet, I found a blue shirt that I thought I had lost and got a fresh pair of socks from my drawer. After slipping into my shoes, I decided that my shoulder where I had tried Olivia's liniment actually felt a lot better.

Dash leapt through the window and onto the table. He looked at me.

"Hungry?" I asked.

He just kept looking at me. I had two cans of tuna fish left. I opened one, spooned half of it onto a small plate, and put it on the floor. Dash went for it, and I finished off what was left, rinsed the can, and threw it in the wastebasket. Then I went to Gunther's room.

"Come in," he called when I knocked.

He was standing near the window, hands clasped behind his back, neat brown suit and tie, looking at me and bouncing on his heels.

"I have found your man," he said.

"My man?"

"The leader of the Nazi cell at Caroll College," he said.

"Who is it?"

"We will know in . . ." he looked at his pocket watch. "Ten minutes."

I sat in the chair I always sat in, one that wasn't too small for me, and leaned back.

"What happens in ten minutes?" I asked.

"A visitor," he said. "You have suffered more injury."

He looked concerned.

"It's a long story," I said. "Well, a medium-length story."

I told him what had happened. Gunther listened, speaking only once to say, "This Joe. He is the leader."

I agreed and finished my tale.

"May I speak?" he asked, still standing.

I nodded.

"You should consider another profession."

"Anita said the same thing."

"The human body is a miracle," he said. "Remarkable but not infinite in its ability to restore itself."

"I know."

"But you will do nothing different?"

"It's what I do," I said. "What would you do if you lost all your clients?"

Gunther thought for a moment and said, "I would live on my savings and investments and write a book on the Kurdish struggle for independence."

"Sounds like best-seller material," I said.

"It would be a labor of scholarship, a much needed treatise and one that would afford me great satisfaction, though my audience would be admittedly limited to scholars."

There was a knock at the door, which opened before Gunther could speak. Mrs. Plaut stood there. I could see someone behind her.

"There's someone here has an appointment with you," she said to Gunther.

"Yes, yes," said Gunther.

"Did you use Olivia's liniment?" she said to me.

"Worked fine," I said.

"You may keep it for future needs. I have fourteen bottles."

"You use it?" I asked.

"Olivia had a gift for curing," she said, "but she also had a belief that cure could not come without pain. I would prefer to suffer than let that liniment touch my body."

"Thanks," I said.

"You are welcome."

Mrs. Plaut went back in the hall, and Gunther's visitor entered. Mrs. Plaut closed the door and I found myself looking up at a familiar face.

"Miss Wright," Gunther said. "Please have a seat."

He gestured toward his desk chair, a chair in which I had never seen anyone but Gunther.

Jacklyn Wright looked at me without expression and sat in the chair. She was wearing a dark green dress and a light green sweater. Her hair was brushed back and her skin looked pink and clean. An all-American look.

She looked at Gunther and said something in German. Gunther answered. They went on for a little while. She started to talk faster, and Gunther was about to say something when I cut him off with, "Hold it. What's going on?"

"Miss Wright wishes some reassurances," Gunther said.

"Reassurances?"

"She is concerned about whether you have sufficient influence to keep her from prison if she agrees to reveal what we need to know."

I thought about Cantwell and D'Argentero, the FBI men, and about Phil.

"Odds are good," I said. "But no guarantees."

"I'll settle, if necessary," she said, "for an opportunity to leave the city if you agree to get rid of the FBI agents who are following me. Within a day, I can be in Canada and have a new identity."

"And start another cell," I said.

"No. We've lost the war. There are only the fanatics, who still believe Hitler can come up with a miracle, and the schemers, who are looking for ways to profit from defeat. Our little cell is a pitiful group waiting for orders that are never going to come."

"We help you and you turn over the guy you report to," I said. "Something's missing."

She looked at me and then turned away.

"He's planning to leave the city sometime late tonight," she said. "He's planning to leave me, all of us for the FBI. He doesn't know that I know, but I do. He tells me he and I will get out together, that he has a plan. He's told me one lie too many."

"Something's still missing," I said.

She sighed.

"We have been lovers," she said. "He plans to simply walk away from me, leave me for the FBI while he takes off with . . ."

"Someone else?" I said.

I had an idea who the someone else was—one or both of the women who had shot at me a few hours earlier.

Her silence answered my question.

"Miss Wright contacted me," Gunther said. "I told her I would hear her offer and relay it to you, but you came here in time and so . . ."

"Did she call you here?" I asked.

"No," said Gunther. "She handed me a note at Freed's Bookstore early this morning."

"I'd been following him," she said. "I follow him. The FBI follows me. I am tired of this war. I am tired of this hiding and intriguing and accomplishing nothing."

"Okay," I said. "Give us what you've got. If it's true, I'll buy you the time to get out. If you're setting us up, I'll go right to the FBI. Why didn't you just set up this deal with them in the first place?"

"I don't trust them," she said. "They would tell me they would make a deal, and then they would not honor it. They've done it before, often. It is the way they work, the way they should work."

We were there now.

"Who are we looking for and where do I find him?"

"He is Lawrence Toddhunter, and he lives on the cliffs overlooking the reservoir over Laurel Canyon," she said.

"Toddhunter?" I asked.

"The dean of the School of Performance at Caroll," Gunther said.

"Yes. He recruited me when I came to apply for a job. He knew my parents were German. I could claim that he seduced me, tricked me, but that would not be true. He convinced me. I am not a fool. Now he plans to run with some information that he hopes to negotiate with if he gets caught."

What I did now was get Toddhunter's address and decide to go find a phone and tell the FBI I didn't want any more of this, and if I messed up again I could find myself with some creative and colorful federal charges against me. After I told the FBI, I'd find a phone that wasn't tapped, as was Mrs. Plaut's, and tell Cary Grant what I had done. It wasn't the way he wanted it, but I'd try to make him see I had no choice.

I got a phone number where I could reach Jacklyn Wright or leave a message. She got up and looked at Gunther and then at me.

"I have your word," she said.

"Yes," Gunther and I said together, and she walked out, almost bumping into Mrs. Plaut, who was on her way in.

"Mr. Peelers," she said. "You have a telephone call."

I followed her into the hall and went to the phone on the landing, watching Jacklyn Wright hurry down the stairs and through the front door.

"Peters," I said, picking up the phone on the landing.

"You just had a visitor," the familiar voice said.

"Did I?"

"You did,"said Joe, who I now knew was Lawrence Toddhunter. "I believe other ears may be listening to us, so I strongly suggest you use no names."

"Go on."

"I have a riddle for you," he said.

"I can't wait to hear it."

"What is short, round, bald, nearsighted, fond of very cheap cigars, and is sitting five feet away from me? Don't give a name. Just answer "yes" if you know the answer."

"Yes," I said.

"Good," he said. "And what is pretty, young, dark, and remarkably calm when faced with terrible danger."

"Yes," I said.

He had Shelly and Violet.

"Excellent," he said. "You will see both of these prizes alive, well fed, and only slightly disheveled sometime tomorrow. They will call you. I have no reason to harm them unless you give me one. All you need do is nothing. Provide no information to individuals or agencies. You understand?"

"Yes," I said.

"Fine, now I expect you will be busy answering the questions of those who are surely listening to our conversation."

"I've got some questions," I said.

"And I probably have answers," he said. "But I have no intention of giving them."

He hung up.

Okay, Peters, I said to myself. In about five or ten minutes the FBI is going to come through the front door, sit you down, and want to know what that telephone conversation was about.

There was a good chance Toddhunter was telling the truth, that he would let Violet and Shelly go. But there was also a better chance that he wouldn't.

Gunther was in the hall now. I told him quickly about the phone call, and he told me that he would reveal none of our conversation with Jacklyn Wright to the FBI.

There was a knock at the front door. I was wrong about how long it would take the FBI to show up. I ran to my room, closed the door, and went to the window. Dash had finished his tuna and gone back outside. I followed him.

I'd gone out this way once before and almost broken my neck. I had to sit on the window ledge, lean over to the branch of a tree, get a good grip, and swing my legs around the thick branch. Then I had to shimmy down toward the trunk and make my way to the ground, finding branches that would hold my weight.

It was harder this time than it had been the last. The last time I had been three years younger and not suffering from a sore shoulder, a stitched scalp, and assorted bruises afforded temporary relief by Olivia's liniment. I didn't look down. It wasn't the height that worried me. It was the possibility of seeing a couple of well-dressed men patiently waiting.

I got to the trunk of the tree. Dash was sitting on a branch, watching me with interest. He got more interested when my hand slipped and I almost fell. I grabbed for anything, got a handful of leaves, and pulled myself back to safety. Dash was no longer interested. He dropped to a lower branch and then to the ground.

I made it to the ground, too, and looked up expecting to see someone in my window, but there was no one there. I ran past the big garage in the yard and went over a low fence into the neighbor's yard. I stepped into a victory garden with a patch of tomatoes. I managed to keep from stepping on the tomatoes and made my way around the house to the street.

There was a big dark car parked in front of Mrs. Plaut's, but there was no driver. The FBI was still inside looking for me. The Crosley was parked half a block away. I dashed for it, got in, and made a tight U-turn. Even if the agents had been in their car, they couldn't have made the turn without some skillful maneuvering.

I was gone and I kept driving. My Crosley was too easy to spot if the FBI at Mrs. Plaut's came looking. I didn't stop till I got to the Melrose Grotto at 5507 Melrose. I went in, ordered a grilled cheese and a beer, got change for a dollar, and went to the pay phone near the door.

The phone rang a dozen times before Grant picked up the phone. I didn't know if his phone was tapped, but it probably was.

"It's Peters," I said.

"What's happening?" he asked.

"A lot," I said. "Can you meet me at the same place we met the first night? Don't mention the name."

"When?"

"When can you get there?" I asked.

"I've got to be at the studio for a meeting," he said.

"Will seven be all right?"

"Fine," I said. "But someone might want to keep you company."

"I'll come alone," he said. "Seven."

"Seven," I confirmed and hung up.

If Grant was being tailed and couldn't manage to shake it, I would need a different game plan. I wasn't sure what it would be.

I was pretty certain the second call I made wouldn't be tapped. It was to my brother at the Wilshire station. I talked to a desk sergeant whose voice I didn't recognize and got put through to Phil, who said quietly, "Where are you?"

"I'm about to have a grilled cheese and a beer."

"The FBI wants to talk to you."

"I know," I said. "I promised to call you if I found my friend Joe. I found him."

Silence from my brother, so I went on.

"There's a problem. He's got Shelly and Violet. He says he'll let them go if I don't tell the FBI or police where he is."

"Where is he?"

"Phil, I . . ."

"He threatened to kill my wife and kids," Phil said. "He'll pay for that. It's not a cop thing, it's a personal one. Besides he's a god-damn Nazi. The FBI gets him and they lock him up, treat him nice, let him give information for favors, and when the war is over, they let him walk. I don't want him walking, Tobias."

"I'm going there to get Shelly and Violet out," I said. "When they're safe, do what you want. I'll give you the address if you promise not to go there till eleven tonight. If I don't have them out by then, I won't be getting them out."

"You have my word," Phil said.

"Good enough."

I gave him the address.

"Anything else?" he asked.

"No, you?"

"Ruth's going back in the hospital Monday," he said angrily. "I don't think she'll be coming out this time."

"What can I do?" I asked.

"Come over this weekend. Bring Anita."

"Sunday," I said. "We'll bring the food if I'm not in a federal prison."

"Sunday'll be fine."

I hung up, and moved to the bar, where I ate my sandwich,

drank my beer, and listened to Woody Herman on the jukebox. There weren't many customers at the Grotto this early. It was kind of odd to feel the dark room swinging to the music with no one jitterbugging or even listening, except me and maybe the bartender, who looked as if what he was whistling was not necessarily what the Woodchoppers were playing.

There were a lot of things I could do now. I could go take a look at Toddhunter's place and see if I could get in. However, he'd would be looking for visitors and I'd probably be pretty easy to spot on this sunny day.

I could take in an afternoon movie, but there was nothing I really wanted to see. So I headed for Riverside Drive, took it to Griffith Park Drive, and parked in the zoo parking lot. Griffith Park is a 3,761-acre slice of hilly land on the easternmost part of the Santa Monica mountains. The park had originally been part of Rancho Los Feliz. It had been donated to the city in 1898 by its last owner, Colonel Griffith J. Griffith.

I walked up one of the low hills on the zoo grounds and went for my favorite spot, the large primate cages. Two gorillas were having their lunch when I reached them. Both were seated, delicately selecting vegetables from a pile on the floor of the cage.

The larger gorilla looked up at me, half a head of lettuce sticking out of his mouth. His eyes met mine. We were kindred spirits. At least, that's what I thought.

When there were no other visitors around, I talked to the gorillas or the chimps. The gorillas paid more attention. I leaned on the railing and looked through the bars.

"I've had a hell of a day," I told the big gorilla.

He kept eating, but he looked at me intelligently. I took it as a sign that he didn't mind if I continued.

"Someone tried to kill me," I said. "Someone is threatening to kill a couple of my friends. A Nazi. I mean the guy holding them who tried to kill me is a Nazi."

"That's how you got all scratched up?" came a raspy voice at my side.

"Yeah."

The gorilla found a banana and delicately peeled it, still looking at me.

"You think *you* had a bad day," came a raspy voice again.

A thin woman in a cloth coat too warm for the afternoon had moved up to the railing without my seeing her. Her hair was white and wild. She had clear light blue eyes and a smooth face. I couldn't tell how old she was. She clutched a big blue purse to her chest.

"I slept in the park, a little shed behind the Greek Theater," she said.

I wasn't sure what to say, so I just nodded and went back to looking at the gorilla. He was now staring at the thin woman.

"Look at them," she said. "Place to sleep every night. Someone feeds 'em. Don't have to work, worry about where the next meal is coming, where to bed down."

"They give up their freedom for that," I said.

She cackled.

"Put me in a cage with a place to sleep and three squares and you can come and talk to me whenever you like about Nazis trying to kill you."

"I was talking to the gorilla. I mean, about the Nazis."

She shrugged and leaned her chin on the purse.

"Go on," she said. "I talk to 'em too. Say, if a cop comes by, don't tell him I tried to put the bite on you."

"You didn't," I said.

"I'm working up to it," she said. "Cop comes and real polite ushers me out of the zoo if I'm puttin' on the bite."

"We're just fellow animal lovers," I said.

"And both maybe a little nuts," she said. "Nazis trying to kill you. You come back from the war shell-shocked, something?"

"Too old for the war," I said.

"So was Milton," she said, "but he volunteered and they took him. Want to know why?"

"Why?" I asked, and the gorilla and I waited for an answer.

"Because he had a special skill, my Milton, which is something I don't got. Milton knew barometers, thermometers, all kinds of meters. Worked for the city. Not this one, Newark, New Jersey. Then he got himself killed on a ship somewhere and left me *bubkas*."

She looked at me.

"Is that a sad story?"

"Very," I said.

"Sad enough to make you kick in a few bucks?" she asked.

"Sad enough," I said, pulling out my wallet and fishing out two singles.

She took them and plunked them into her purse.

"That's one of my better stories," she said. "Depends on the customer which story I use. True story is even too sad for me to tell myself. Won't tell that one for five, even ten bucks. Rather starve. This is the point where you tell me you gotta go. You're late for something."

"I'm not late for anything," I said.

She was looking at the gorilla again.

"Got any kids?" she asked softly.

"No."

"Good," she said. "You lose 'em, you lose your heart. Know what I mean?"

"I think so," I said.

"Gorillas," she said, looking back at the two animals. "They look so smart. Like they're thinking, working out some big problem. You think?"

"Maybe."

"Maybe," she repeated and ran a hand through her wild hair. "Listen, I gotta go get something to eat. It's been good talkin' to you."

"Same here," I said.

"And stay away from those Nazis. They're bad news."

She walked away, a slight limp. I watched her head down the hill, her eyes toward the ground. I looked at the gorilla. He was watching her too.

"You could have offered her a carrot," I said.

He picked up a green pepper and popped it into his mouth. A couple with two little kids was coming up the hill toward me. The woman with the wild white hair and cloth coat stopped them. I wondered what story she was telling them.

CHAPTER 15

I GOT TO Wally's at six-thirty. Wally, behind the bar, recognized me and nodded toward the back booth near the washrooms. Grant wasn't there yet.

"What'll it be?" Wally asked as I sat down.

"You got soup?"

"Clam chowder," he said. "Or Mexican bean."

"Chowder."

He nodded and wandered off. I had my .38 in my pocket. It felt solid.

I was finished with my chowder and working on my second beer of the day when Cary Grant appeared and sat across from me. He was wearing gray slacks and a gray turtleneck shirt with a flecked sports jacket.

"Well?" he asked.

"You sure no one followed you?"

"I'm sure someone started to," he said. "But I'm also pretty sure I lost them in the hills. Tell me what's going on and where you got those scratches."

I brought him up to date. He listened quietly and nodded at all the right places.

"Amazing," he said, sitting back.

"I'm going to Toddhunter's to try to save my friends," I said. "You stay here. I'll call if something goes wrong and I can get to a phone. Then you can . . ."

"No," he said.

"No?"

"I'm going with you," said Grant.

"I don't want to be responsible for getting Cary Grant killed."

"And Cary Grant doesn't wish to get killed. But this is something I want to do. You sure there's no other way?"

"We can wait, let Toddhunter get away, and hope he lets my friends go."

Grant shook his head "no."

"We can call in the cops and the FBI and raid the place," I said.

"Which might get your friends killed."

"Might," I said.

"All right, when do we go?"

"When it's definitely dark."

Grant ordered a drink and asked me about myself. I told stories for about an hour and a half, and he encouraged me. I considered another beer but didn't go for it. I don't take alcohol well, but I do take aspirin well and popped some and a couple of the doc's pills into my mouth.

Grant asked Wally if we could leave my car in his parking lot for a while.

"Long as you want," Wally said. "Nobody'll bother it. Leave it all night if you want."

Grant drove. His car was a black Cadillac that smelled new and felt like it was barely moving when he hit fifty miles an hour going onto the canyon road.

"We should have a plan," he said.

"We should," I agreed.

"I mean something besides 'let's climb a wall, run in, save your friends, and hold Toddhunter for the FBI.'"

Since that had been my plan, I just said, "Uh huh. Let's see what the place looks like when we get there. They might have dogs."

"Yes," he said. "I wouldn't care for that."

The driveway to Toddhunter's house was to our left as we made our way to the top of the road heading toward the San Fernando Valley. The driveway was clearly marked with a sign, black numbers on a white background, topped with a cute wrought iron outline of a girl in a bonnet pouring what was probably milk for a waiting dog.

Grant pulled off to the side to let a couple of cars pass us and found a space a few yards off the road under a sagging tree.

We got out. It was dark, but there was a half-moon and a clear sky. I had the .38 in one pocket and my small flashlight in the other. We waited till there was no traffic and crossed the road.

The driveway was narrow, covered in crushed stone, leading into the darkness. Maybe forty or fifty yards down, there were some lights. We headed for them, keeping to the right side. Our footsteps crunched on the crushed stone.

No dogs barked. A good sign.

We came to a stone wall. Not a good sign.

The wall was about eight feet high.

We inched our way along the wall into bramble and small boulders. I held my flashlight low, leading the way. We came to a stop when we hit the end of the wall. There was nowhere to go but down, straight down into the canyon.

"The other way," Grant whispered.

We went back past a solid wooden gate as high as the wall and moved to the left. It turned out to be pretty much the same as the other side. Toddhunter's house was on a piece of land over the reservoir, a plot surrounded on three sides by a drop into the canyon and on the other side by a tall stone wall.

"Well," said Grant. "I guess we go over."

"Might be wire or glass up there," I said.

"You've got the bad arm," he said. "Get on my shoulders and take a look."

I tried to think of another way, even considered ringing the bell and saying something like, "You're surrounded. Give up while you can." It never worked for David Harding, Counterspy, on the radio, so I doubted it would work for Toby Peters. With David Harding, at least, the command was usually true.

Grant bent his knees and held out his hand to me. I pocketed the flashlight, took his hand, and put my palm against the stone wall expecting to topple backwards as he stood up. I didn't know if he could stand up under my one hundred seventy or so pounds.

He didn't even wobble. I put my hands carefully on the top of the wall and looked over. No glass or wire. The wall was about a foot thick. Beyond it about thirty more yards was a ranch-style house. There were lights on, and I saw someone move in front of a window, pause, and look out into the night in my general direction but not right at me. It was Miss Jones, the young redhead. She had a drink in one hand, a gun in the other, and a look on her face I couldn't read from this distance.

"Well?" asked Grant.

"No dogs," I said. "No wire. No glass."

"Can you climb up there?"

"Someone's . . ." I started, but Miss Jones turned and walked back away from the window. "Yeah."

"Then do it," Grant said. "My left foot is beginning to slip."

I leaned over the wall and threw my right leg up. The good thing was that it took all of my weight off of Grant. The bad thing was that I almost toppled over the wall. I reached back and grabbed for rough stone and kept from dropping.

"You all right?" Grant whispered.

"Yeah."

"Can you reach down and get me up?"

I straddled the top of the wall as if I were riding a horse, grabbed the edge of the wall with my left hand, and reached down with my right.

"Can you see my hand?"

"Yes," he said. "I'll have to jump a little to reach you. Have you got a good grip?"

"Let's do it," I said.

His hand grabbed my wrist and I held tight to keep from falling. He swung himself up with a quick move and sat next to me on the wall.

"Nice little house," he said. "Let's take a look."

He jumped down and I carefully dangled as far as I could and made the drop. My shoulder felt the impact but it wasn't bad. If I could stop doing things like this for a week or two, I'd probably recover.

We didn't talk. Grant led the way, crouching, trying to stay out of the light from the windows. We made it to the house, and I peeked in the window where I had seen Miss Jones. The light was on. I saw a bed, two night tables, a dresser, and a large painting of a horse on the wall. Otherwise, the room was empty. We worked our way back past the front door and found a dimly lit game room complete with pool table and a dart board. No one was in that room, either.

Grant motioned for me to follow him around the right side of the house. We moved slowly, trying not to make noise and almost succeeding. From the side of the house we could, if we wanted to, look out toward the lights of the valley. Before the war, the valley would have glowed like a Christmas tree, but the blackout had reduced the scene below to a few isolated spots of light.

We worked our way around and got lucky.

Grant was ahead of me. He looked into a lighted room, ducked his head back, and motioned for me to move ahead of him. He pointed to the window and I peeked inside.

Violet was seated on a twin bed. Shelly was on the one next to it. At the door in front of them, on a chair facing them sat the young man who had been dressed as a soldier, the one whose Walther I had taken. Soldier had a magazine on his lap and a fresh gun in his hand. He also had a large white bandage taped over his left eye where I'd slammed it into the toilet.

We ducked under the window frame and kept going. Through the window of the next room we saw Lawrence Toddhunter and the two women. It was a large living room, beyond which we could see a dining room. Toddhunter was checking three suitcases to be sure they were securely tight. Miss Smith stood drinking nervously, and Miss Jones kept checking her watch.

One of the women said something. I couldn't make it out, but we did hear Toddhunter's answer.

"Stop checking. We'll get the call precisely on time and then we can leave."

"And those two?" asked Miss Jones, motioning toward the closed bedroom door where Shelly and Violet were.

"We can see if they can fly," said Toddhunter.

"Why can't we just tie them up and lock them in a closet?" she said.

Toddhunter stopped securing the luggage and looked at her.

"Because, my dear, we have not been particularly discreet in discussing our plans in front of them."

Miss Smith nodded in agreement.

Grant and I moved back from the window and out of sight.

"What now?" he asked.

I was the professional. I was the one who was supposed to come up with a plan. At first, all I could think of was breaking the bedroom window, shooting the soldier, and taking a few shots at the door to keep Toddhunter and the two women from rushing in.

The problem with that plan was that I'm a terrible shot, even with my own .38. It was also possible that by the time I got the window broken, the soldier would shoot me and Grant and probably use Violet and Shelly for target practice, just to keep up his skills.

Before I could decide what to do, Grant said, "I think I've got it. I'll get him out of the room. You try to get through the window. I'll stall them. You go out there through the bedroom door."

"And do what?"

"Save my life," said Grant, scurrying past me.

I moved back to the bedroom window and waited. After about twenty seconds, I heard the distant sound of a door chime. The soldier put down his magazine. A few seconds later, I heard voices from the living room. One of the voices was Cary Grant's. Soldier hesitated, looked at Violet and Shelly, and then got up, still holding his gun, and went through the bedroom door, leaving it open behind him so he could keep an eye on his prisoners.

I stepped directly in front of the window and tried to open it. It was locked from the inside. I tapped at the window. Violet, on the bed nearest the window, looked at me and then back at the open door. I motioned to the window lock. She got up slowly and hurried to the window. The voices from the living room were louder now.

Violet pushed the latch and together we opened the window. Shelly, who had been oblivious to all of this, squinted in our direction through his thick glasses. A look of hope, but not certainty, touched his round face.

I climbed in carefully with Violet's help. Shelly started to get up but I motioned him back. He was in a direct line to the open door. If someone looked in, they would see him move and we'd have company and chaos.

I motioned for Violet to follow me along the wall behind the chair where Soldier had been sitting. Through the open door, we could hear Toddhunter saying, "It's too late, Mr. Grant. Or perhaps it's still too early. I don't have to bargain with you over what I have while I still have the opportunity to get away."

"The police and the FBI are right outside," Grant said calmly. "There's no way out but that driveway, and you'd have to get through a wave of bullets that might prove inconveniencing."

"You are bluffing," Toddhunter said.

"Am I?"

"Even if you are not, I have three very useful hostages. The repulsive fat dentist, the young woman, and now a very famous actor. Miss Jones, get our two guests."

Violet was closest to the door. Miss Jones came in, gun in hand, looking at Shelly, whose eyes were wide with fear. Miss Jones looked over at Violet's empty bed, sensed the movement to her left, and started to turn.

Violet, who was not the wife of Rocky Gonsenelli for nothing, hit her with a stiff left to the midsection and a right to the jaw. Miss Jones crumpled forward, and Violet picked up the gun she had dropped.

"Shelly," I called and waved.

He looked at the open door and clambered out of the bed just as a shot came into the room and slammed into the wall about where he'd been sitting. Shelly panted his way to my side. Miss Jones tried to get up. Violet put her down with a long-count right cross.

"We've got her gun," I called out. "And mine."

"And I've got Cary Grant," Toddhunter answered. "I suggest we work something out."

"Watch out, Toby," Grant said. "The other man just went out the back."

"We leave here with Grant," Toddhunter said. "You stay where you are with your friends. We let Grant go when we're safely away."

"Don't believe them," Grant said. "And look out for . . ."

Violet swung around, with the gun and fired at the bedroom window. Shelly let out a yelp. Soldier stood outside the window, a bewildered look on his face and a splotch of blood on his chest. He swayed back and then toppled forward into the bedroom with a loud thud.

"Wait till I tell Rocky I got one," she said.

"Your man is dead!" I called out. "Jones is out cold."

"My offer still stands," Toddhunter said. "Nothing has changed. You can have a stupid gun battle in which Grant will definitely be the first to die, or you can deal. I really don't have much time."

"Give me a second," I said and motioned to Violet that I was heading for the window.

I climbed over the soldier's body and went through the window as quietly as I could. I moved back to the living room window and looked in carefully. Toddhunter and Miss Smith were side by side. Toddhunter was aiming a gun at Grant, who stood with his hands in his pockets.

I kept moving around the house. The soldier had come out that way. I could go in. I found an open door that led into a kitchen.

"I'm waiting, Peters," Toddhunter said. "Impatiently."

I eased my way through the kitchen and found myself in the doorway looking at the backs of Smith and Toddhunter. Grant saw me but gave nothing away. What I should have done at that point was shoot Toddhunter in the back, and possibly Smith, too, though she didn't have a gun.

"Drop the gun," I said. "Don't turn around."

That seemed a reasonable thing to say, but reason was not operating in this house. Panic took over. Toddhunter wheeled and fired in my direction. He hit the refrigerator, which started to scream. I fired too, but I hit the ceiling. Plaster fell. Toddhunter aimed at me again. This time I fell forward to the floor and lost my gun.

Grant jumped on Toddhunter, but Smith grabbed his arm and Toddhunter turned to push Grant back so he could get a good shot at him. As Smith grabbed for my .38, Violet got a shot off from the bedroom that stopped Toddhunter long enough for Grant to make a dash for the front door. Toddhunter turned and fired toward the bedroom. I got up fast and went out the back door, with the woman who now had my gun about a dozen steps behind me.

I turned left, heading toward nothing but the edge of the grounds which dropped off to the end of the world. Behind me I heard noise, lots of noise, and gunfire. I was running now. A wrong turn and I'd vanish down into the canyon.

Something suddenly changed. I wasn't sure what. I looked back and saw that Smith wasn't following me. She was running back toward the house.

I nearly stepped into a small swimming pool, danced around it, and almost collided with Cary Grant.

"What's happening?" I asked.

"I don't know," he said. "But Toddhunter's right behind me."

A shot zinged into the night above our heads. From the light of the house, I could see Toddhunter heading our way. He didn't seem to be in any hurry. We had no place to run but the ledge to nowhere, which is exactly what we did.

It was then we started our climb down into darkness. It was then that Grant reached down to help me up and I grabbed his wrist. It was then that the beam of a flashlight in Toddhunter's hand lit our faces as Toddhunter began prying lose Grant's grip on the rock above him. It was then that I began to loose my sweaty grip on his wrist and start imagining the headlines in which I would be a small footnote to a front-page story about the dramatic death of Cary Grant.

It was also then that the flashlight beam wavered and the flashlight came tumbling into the darkness past my head, spinning as it fell. About a second later, the flashlight was followed by the hurtling Lawrence Toddhunter, who came close to hitting me and taking me with him into the blackness of the reservoir below.

"Can't hold on," I said.

"Just a few seconds longer," Grant said and pulled me up abruptly.

Someone had taken Grant's arm and grabbed him back with me dangling below him. That "someone" stood at the rim of the reservoir now, looking at both of us.

"You all right?" asked Phil.

"Alive," I said.

"Cary Grant," I said. "This is my brother, Phil. He's a cop."

"Pleased to meet you," said Grant. "No, I am elated to meet you."

Phil moved to take a look over the rim toward where Toddhunter's body had fallen.

"He's the one who said he'd kill Ruth and the kids?" my brother said.

"Yes."

Phil turned and led the way back to the house. The two women were both in handcuffs, being held by uniformed cops. Violet was calming Shelly, who was saying, "I'm fine. I'm fine."

"You sure?" asked Violet.

"No, but I'm fine. That's what you're supposed to say. That's what I'm saying. I'm fine."

"Can we go now?" Grant asked.

"The FBI will want to talk to you," said Phil.

"They'll know where to find me," Grant said, picking up the briefcase that stood next to the suitcases near the hallway. "My briefcase. You mind?"

"No," said Phil.

"The FBI might . . ." Grant started.

"Let them," said Phil. "Let them."

EPILOGUE

ANITA AND I went to the movies. We saw *This Is The Army*, a Movietone Newsreel, a *Time Marches On*, and a Donald Duck cartoon, *In The Fuhrer's Face*. We had a nice dinner, thanks to a two-hundred-dollar bonus from Cary Grant, who had called me the day after the shoot-out and said that the briefcase contained the material he needed—a list of names he had already turned over to the right people.

The FBI never came to see me. I'm not sure why.

Jacklyn Wright disappeared. Shelly went back to his dental practice with a newfound respect for Violet, who took advantage of having saved her boss's life by asking him for a raise. This request Shelly immediately granted.

On the morning Anita and I went to the movie and dinner, I had gone through Shelly's office and heard him telling a dazed little man how he had captured a den of Nazi spies.

A week later at breakfast in Mrs. Plaut's dining room, the phone rang upstairs. Gunther, who was expecting a call, hurried to get it.

"More avocado pancakes?" Mrs. Plaut asked.

We all politely declined, though I thought they tasted pretty good if you didn't put the jalapeno syrup on them.

Gunther came hurrying back to the dining room to announce that the call was for me from Shelly. I excused myself and made my way up the stairs. My wounds had pretty much healed. The stitches had been removed from my head, and I had picked up a few extra dollars between cases by filling in for the house detective at the Roosevelt Hotel.

"Hello, Shel, what's up?"

"I'm in jail," he moaned.

He began to sob. I've heard Sheldon Minck sob before. It's not a pretty sound, but this time it sounded more genuine than any time in the past.

"What did you do?"

"Nothing," he cried. "But Mildred's dead. My dear Mildred's dead. And they think I killed her."

"Then you've got nothing to worry about, Shel. I'll call Marty Leib and . . ."

"You don't understand, Toby. They have a witness who says she saw me do it."

"Sheldon, who says they saw you kill Mildred?"

"Joan Crawford," he said.